candy apple books...
just for you.
sweet. fresh. fun.
take a bite!

Snowfall Surprise

Snowfall Surprise

by Jane B. Mason
and Sarah Hines Stephens

SCHOLASTIC INC.

New York Toronto London Auckland Sydney
Mexico City New Delhi Hong Kong Buenos Aires

No part of this publication may be reproduced, stored in a retrieval system, or transmitted in any form or by any means, electronic, mechanical, photocopying, recording, or otherwise, without written permission of the publisher. For information regarding permission, write to Scholastic Inc., Attention: Permissions Department, 557 Broadway, New York, NY 10012.

ISBN-13: 978-0-545-10067-0
ISBN-10: 0-545-10067-4

12 11 10 9 8 7 6 5 4 3 2 1   9 10 11 12 13 14/0
Printed in the U.S.A.   40
First printing, October 2009

To the generous Jones family, with thanks for all the cabin memories. — SHS

To Nora, Elliot, and Oliver, for being troopers and a lot of fun on the slopes. — JBM

Table of Contents

Chapter 1

Bluebird!

Powderbowl Snowcast:
Storm Advisory! Overnight snow expected Thursday,
heavy at times with temperatures dropping to the mid-
teens. Thirty inches of new snow expected by Friday;
clearing on Saturday and into the week.

Perfect! Savannah Heglund reread the report on the computer screen, then hit speed dial number four on the kitchen phone.

"Hello?"

"Lucy! You aren't going to believe it. It's a ten-foot pack and they're getting thirty inches of fresh pow as we speak. It'll be perfect crud by the time we get up there, and bluebird for the entire week!" she said, talking a mile a minute.

"Savannah? Is that you?" Lucy sounded confused. "What language are you speaking?"

Savannah could picture Lucy, her blue eyes squinched, her dark brows knit. She was undoubtedly flipping her shiny, brown hair to one side and scowling as it fell back to cover one eye, which it always did. Lucy hated to be left out of anything, even lingo, and, in her excitement, Savannah had forgotten that her friend was a winter sport newbie — this was going to be her first real snow trip. Savvy needed to slow down and include a full translation.

"Sorry," Savvy giggled. She slipped her leg up onto a stool beside the family computer, plucked at a thread in her jeans, and started over. "What I meant to say is, the conditions are going to be amazing! There's already a good snow base, that's the pack, and it's snowing great big goose-feather flakes as we speak. The new fluffy stuff is powder or pow, and when it's worked a little so it's just right, it's crud, which sounds bad but is really, really good. The report said the weather is supposed to clear up on Sunday so it'll be all fresh snow and clear skies and that's what you call bluebird conditions — absolutely perfect for us to ski in. Or board in. Or sled in. Or skate in. Or —"

"Okay. Okay, I get it, Snowbunny," Lucy interrupted with a laugh. "Is there anything you *don't* like to do in snow, er, crud?"

Savannah twirled one of her auburn curls around her finger while she thought about that. In her entire eleven years she hadn't met a winter sport she didn't like. And she'd definitely met a lot of them. Her family had a cabin near Lake Tahoe that her dad had been going to since he was a boy. Savvy and her older brother, Avery, had been spending weekends in the snow since before they could walk. According to her dad, Savvy was up on skis at age three (her mom called her the "kamikaze toddler" because she liked to schuss straight downhill with no poles), and was snowboarding by six. According to her brother, Savvy spent most of her time on her face until she was nine, which was when she got good enough to smoke him on the slopes.

It was hard for Savvy to remember for sure what she did when. What she *did* remember were winters full of sliding, swooshing, stomping, and shredding weekends. From November until spring, the Heglunds would pile into their four-wheel-drive station wagon almost every Friday night and head up the hill. Come Sunday, they would drive down the mountain, tired and happy.

Savvy's mom called their winter trips "slip-away weekends." Savvy called them fun. Slip-aways were a complete blast, but even better than taking two days off to play in the snow was taking a whole week off, which they did once a year in the middle of February. Not only did it provide maximum slope time, but Savvy's birthday was also in mid-February, making ski-week a double treat.

"Ooh, I know!" Savvy suddenly remembered the one thing she didn't like to do in snow. "Nothing!" she blurted. It sounded sarcastic, but Savvy was serious. The worst slip-away weekend on record was like a scar in her memory. It had happened last January when it rained, and not just some light, misting rain that made the snow icy either. Big sloppy drops had fallen from the sky for two days straight and turned Savannah's fun into muddy sludge. She'd been marooned in the cabin with nothing to entertain herself but books left over from past summer vacations.

"So, um, what if 'nothing' is the one thing I turn out to be good at?" Lucy asked. Savvy could tell she was trying to make a joke, but Lucy could not hide the nervousness behind it. Savannah's supersmart friend had never so much as strapped on a pair of ski — or snowboard — boots. She was a valley girl through and through, a flatlander. And while she loved to try new things, she also liked to be good at whatever she did. Savvy knew that Lucy was worried that she wouldn't be able to keep up with Savvy and their other BFF, Ellison.

"Lu, don't worry. You're going to be great. Remember, Ellison's no hotdogger either. She's only been skiing a few times. Just focus on packing your suitcase, and I'll show you everything you need to know when we get there."

"Packing I can handle!" Lucy replied with her usual gusto. "And speaking of which . . . I'd better get back to it. I'll see you tomorrow!"

After setting the phone on its cradle and making sure the snow report hadn't been updated in the last six minutes, Savvy tromped down the hall to her bedroom. She surveyed the big purple herringbone duffel on the bed — her own packing in progress — and scooped up the sweater from the top of the pile. The moss-colored turtleneck brought out the green in her hazel eyes, but it looked terrible with her new all-weather shell and made her curly auburn hair look kind of orangey. Bleh. She tossed the sweater back on the closet shelf, grabbed a white one instead, and wondered for the twelfth time if there was anything she'd forgotten.

She had sweaters and wicking layers. Snow

pants and a jacket. Underwear and pajamas. She'd already tossed in cute clothes for the Powderbowl lodge and heavy-duty stuff in case the weather got really crazy (which was known to happen — it was the Sierras, after all). She threw extra gloves, sunglasses, and a pair of ski socks on top. Since the car was small and they went to the Bowl so often, the rest of her gear lived at the cabin. Which reminded her . . .

"Hey, Avery!" Savannah shouted down the hall. "Can Ellison borrow your board?"

Savvy's brother poked his head out into the hall and pulled out one of his earbuds. His faux-hawk was the same rosy brown as Savannah's hair, and though she would never admit it, they also shared the same smattering of freckles, wide smile, and upturned nose. If he wasn't a good five inches taller and three years older, they could have been twins. "What?" Avery asked rudely. Lately, he acted put out if Savannah even spoke to him. Apparently, after you hit fourteen having a younger sister was kind of like having gum on your shoe. Or worse.

"I said, 'can Ellison borrow your board?'" Savvy repeated slower and louder.

"Not a chance," Avery answered quickly, and flashed a fake smile. Savvy thought he was just being mean until he reached into his room and pulled the edge of his board into the hall to show her that it was here at home, which presumably meant he was taking it with him to Colorado, where he and the high school ski team were spending the week.

"Thanks, anyway." Savvy shrugged and stepped back into her room. With Avery and his board out of the picture, Lucy and Ellison would have to rent all their equipment, but in Savvy's mind it was still a win, win, win situation.

Win #1 — Avery *wasn't* going to Powderbowl.

Win #2 — Lucy *was* going to Powderbowl.

Win #3 — Ellison was going to Powderbowl, *too!*

It was such a good stroke it went beyond luck. And though she hated to admit it, Avery was the key. His school ski plans were making her birthday dream a reality.

Usually, with only five seats in the car and four family members, neither Savvy nor her brother got to take friends on slip-away weekends or ski-week. Family-only slip-aways didn't bother Savannah. But ski-week? Her birthday? With no friends? Savvy had lobbied long and hard, and more than once, to bring a buddy with them during the February break. But her parents maintained that it wouldn't be fair to Avery if they both couldn't bring guests. And there wasn't enough room for everyone. Besides the five-seat car limitation, the cabin had only two bedrooms.

But this year, with Avery out of the family ski-week picture, Savannah saw her chance to fill not just one seat, but two. Which was absolutely perfect since she had two best friends.

Flopping down on the bed beside her bag and hitting speed dial three, Savvy put the phone to her ear and waited for Ellison to pick up. The phone only rang once.

"Hey, Sav. I'm already at sunglasses," Ellison answered, talking fast and referring to the alphabetized packing list Savannah had typed up, printed out, and given her friends. "Did you forget to put something on the list? 'Cause if you did, tell me now. I'm running out of room fast."

If Lucy was all in her head, Ellison was all over the place! She had more energy than a pack of Jack Russell terriers and hardly ever stopped moving . . . or talking. Whenever the three friends went to the movies, Savvy and Lucy brought extra gum to keep Ellison's jaw busy. If they didn't, she would blather her way through the film. And if they could get away with it they would probably strap her down to keep her from fidgeting, too.

"I wasn't calling to hassle you about the list," Savvy explained. She'd made sure the packing instructions she gave both of her friends on Monday were thorough.

"You weren't calling about the list? Aren't you packing? I mean, we're still leaving Saturday morning, right?"

Savvy could practically see Ellison's low, sandy-colored ponytails swishing as she talked. And she could actually *hear* her pacing her room.

"Of course we're still going, and I'm all packed, so don't panic. I was calling to tell you Avery brought his board home. He's taking it with him to Colorado."

"Right. So it's rental city for me, then."

"'Fraid so."

"Well, that's no biggie. I'm still not sure if I want to ski or board, anyway. Maybe I'll do both. Not at the same time, of course, unless — do people do that? Maybe I'll just sl —"

Savannah couldn't help but laugh. "Ellison! We're going for a whole week. We can do it all! And we don't have to do it all at once either. We can focus on one thing at a time."

"Right," Ellison said. Savvy heard her inhale slowly.

"See you tomorrow, okay?" Savvy asked.

"You got it," Ellison replied.

Savannah hung up the phone, squeezed everything into her duffel, and sat on it to get it zipped. Tomorrow was going to be the start of the best ski-week ever — birthday, best friends, and seven days of bluebird!

Chapter 2

Digging In

"On the road again . . ."

Savannah moaned and let her head fall back against the seat of the car. "Dad. No singing! You promised," she complained. Her father was a notorious car singer . . . and also notoriously tone deaf, which is why she'd made him swear not to attempt to carry a tune while her friends were in the vehicle. Nothing made the almost three-hour trip feel more like a ten-and-a-half-hour trip than off-key oldies.

"Just getting it out of my system, sweetie," her dad reassured her as they pulled up in front of Lucy's house. *"The life I love is makin' music with my friends, and I can't wait to get on the road again,"* he belted out. "There. All done."

Savvy's mom gave her husband a round of applause that he graciously accepted, slipping his cap off and bowing his balding head.

"Mom, please don't encourage him," Savvy begged in a low voice, half closing her eyes. Lucy was going to be in the car with them any second.

"Sorry, honey. You're right. The last thing we need is an encore." Savvy's mom gave her a wink, then leaned over and kissed her husband on the cheek before climbing out to help Lucy load her bag. "Hi, Lucy. What have you got in here? The whole library?" Savvy's mom hefted the duffel into the back of the wagon with a grunt and closed the hatch.

Lucy smiled, flipped her bangs out of her eyes, and climbed into the car. "Just a few books, Mrs. Heglund. You know, in case."

Savannah eyed her friend's supercute jeans and long-sleeved raspberry hoodie as she closed the station wagon door. "In case what?"

"In case I end up doing a lot of reading, you know, back at the cabin." Lucy shot her friend a sideways glance from under her bangs, and then focused every ounce of her attention on her seat belt as they pulled out of the drive and headed to Ellison's house.

Savvy patted Lucy's arm reassuringly. "You're talking crazy," she said. "Look, you're a fast learner, and I'm a great teacher. Oh. And let's not forget about my friend Eric," she said. "He's always got great tips."

"The one who lives up there?" Lucy did the hair flip and, for a second, Savvy saw both of her eyes.

"That's the one," Savvy confirmed with a grin. "He's an amazing skier and an excellent boarder, too. He totally rips."

"Who rips? What? What did I miss?" The car had stopped at the end of the block. Ellison had already yanked open Savvy's door and was leaning inside. She motioned for Savvy to shove over.

Savannah started to scoot, then stopped and raised her hands in surrender. "I just want to say that I am only willing to ride the hump because Lucy hasn't really been to the snow before and deserves a good view, and, even more importantly, Ellison barfs on car trips."

"Big of you, Sav." Ellison nodded as she slipped out of her soft, pink fleece jacket. "But I feel it is my duty to inform you that you are making the right choice."

"I'll say," Lucy agreed, her blue eyes full of mischief. "Remember how sorry I was on the bus back from Six Flags?" Lucy shuddered at the memory, and all three girls cracked up. Nobody could forget that day. After seven roller coasters and a two-hour car ride, Ellison's stomach had launched a major protest . . . all over Lucy's Keds.

When they stopped laughing, Ellison jabbed Savvy in the ribs lightly with her elbow. "That is one present you definitely don't want for your birthday."

As the station wagon drove through the valley, fields, nut trees, and shopping centers gave way to pines, manzanita bushes, and mountain views. In the backseat, Savvy excitedly told her friends all about Powderbowl.

"It's the prettiest resort in the Sierras," she said. "They call it 'Powderbowl' because it gets the most powder and it's shaped like a giant bowl with steep sides."

"How steep?" Lucy asked.

"Not too steep, Luce, I promise," Savvy assured her. "There are plenty of beginner runs. Remember, my friend Eric started skiing there when he was two!"

"Two?" her friends echoed.

"Yup. His great-grandfather opened the resort, like, seventy-five years ago, and it's been in the family ever since. Eric grew up on the mountain. We met when I was really little, when he tore by me on Finder's Folly, my first blue square run. I took off after him, but he beat me to the bottom . . . barely. I think that's when he gave me the nickname 'Shredder.'"

"Shredder?" Ellison repeated.

Lucy laughed. "Not exactly a pretty name, is it?"

"No, but it's a total compliment," Savvy assured them. "My friend Hector says that the snowboard I've picked out is for serious shredders only, like me." Savannah grinned and looked out the window. The higher they climbed, the deeper the snow . . . until it was up to the tops of the orange snow poles that marked the edge of the highway and guided the huge plows during storms.

Savannah had driven this route so many times she knew the way by heart, but seeing it fresh through her friends' eyes made it extra exciting, and she anticipated each approaching curve.

"I think we're going to have to do some digging," Savvy's dad announced as they turned off the highway onto the small road that led to the cabin.

"To build a snow fort?" Lucy asked.

"No, to get inside!" Savvy bounced up and down in her seat as she stared through the front windshield. They'd arrived at last, and the cabin was nearly buried in snow! Icicles clung to the edges of the roof, some of them touching the drifts that reached more than halfway up the windows. The driveway had been plowed, but the path to the door and the door itself were covered in white.

Mrs. Heglund pulled out the shovel they carried in the car (you never knew when you might need a shovel in the Sierras), and started in while the girls *ooh*ed and *aah*ed and got out their puffy, warm jackets, hats, and gloves.

Once they were warmish, the girls picked up the extra shovels Savvy's dad had pulled from the lean-to and pitched in. With everyone shoveling it didn't take long to make a wide path to the house. They were almost to the door when Savvy heard a shout.

"Incoming!" came the muffled call.

Savvy should have noticed that her dad had disappeared. From the other side of the cabin a large snowball sailed up and over the peak of the roof, landing somewhere in the middle of the sloped plane above them and releasing a shower of snow. Savvy jumped back, but too late. A thick wall of white slid off the green metal roof and covered her in chilly powder. A pile of frozen fluff balanced on her knit pom-pom hat, a clump seeped into the neck of her coat, and flakes even dusted her eyelashes. Everyone else had stepped back in time.

Ellison doubled over. "You look like a snowman," she said between peals of laughter. Lucy and Mrs. Heglund were cracking up, too.

"That's snow*woman* to you," Savvy corrected. She pulled a handful of snow out of her collar and launched it at Ellison, landing a direct hit. Lucy started cracking up harder and Ellison lobbed the next icy grenade at her, which notched her laughing up to full-blown hysterics. Seconds later, snow was flying in all directions.

Distracted, Savvy almost let her dad get away. Luckily, she spotted him out of the corner of her eye, hiding behind one of the puzzle-bark pine trees that surrounded the little house. He was trying to make his way back to the car and cover, ducking from trunk to trunk. With speed and precision, Savvy began lobbing snowballs his way, landing several hits. Caught in the deep snow, her dad couldn't run. While he struggled to get away, Savvy called on her friends for backup. Her mom happily joined in, too, and before long, Savvy's dad was completely iced, lying in a drift, and holding up a single glove in surrender.

"Okay, Frosty. We'll let you go. But that means you're on fire duty," Savvy's mom announced. "*And* you have to finish digging."

The lump of white moaned, then struggled to his feet and grinned. "It was worth it," he declared as he tried to shake the snow from his body.

It only took a few more shovelfuls of snow to clear the door, and the cabin was open.

"Come on." Savvy stomped her boots and waved her friends in. "Keep your coats on," she advised. "It's cold in here."

Everyone stepped inside and Savvy showed them around. The pine-log cabin was small, with a living room, dining room, bath, and kitchen downstairs, and another bath and two bedrooms on the second floor. The bigger bedroom had been dubbed "the dorm" by Savvy's grandparents when the cabin was built. It was long and narrow and Savvy's favorite room. Because it was on the second floor, the ceiling was peaked in the middle, matching the line of the roof. It had dormer windows pushing out on both sides and vintage ski posters on the walls. There were two twin beds (formerly belonging to her dad and Aunt Tilly — now hers and Avery's) and a trundle they could pull out to make a third bed between them.

"Wow. This is so great," Ellison announced, dropping her bag on the wide plank floor. "I can see why you love it here." From the largest of the windows, there was a view of the lake and the snow-covered mountains surrounding it. The sun, which had stayed away all day, peeked out from a single stretch of clear sky between the clouds and the earth, creating an Alpine sunset beautiful enough to silence Savvy's chatty friend.

Lucy didn't see the view. She was staring wide-eyed at one of the posters — a '70s guy jumping moguls and spraying powder out in a rooster tail behind him. As she stared, she chewed her finger-nail nervously. Savannah was pretty sure she knew what her friend was thinking, and wished she could set her mind at ease. But before she could get a word out, her mother's voice rang through the cabin.

"Hot chocolate!" she called up from the kitchen. The Heglunds were so practiced at cabin living it only took twenty minutes to unload food, turn on water, and check pipes for damage. Usually by the time the milk for cocoa was hot, they had a fire laid and were ready to relax before dinner.

The girls tromped down the stairs to collect their steamy, marshmallow-topped mugs and huddle around the fire. The chill in the living room air was already beginning to dissipate.

Savvy stripped off her jacket and wrapped her hands around her mug, basking in the glow of the burning logs and her friends' company. The trip was everything she'd hoped so far and they were just warming up! They hadn't even had dinner . . . ooohh, dinner. Suddenly, Savvy had an idea.

First nights in the cabin the Heglunds almost always stayed in and had something easy, like soup and grilled cheese sandwiches. But tonight Savvy was anxious to show her friends a little more.

"Mom, I know you're probably tired from all that unpacking. So I was thinking —"

"Lodge for dinner?" her mom asked with a knowing smile, and Savvy beamed back. She'd gotten her wish again, and she hadn't even had to mention the word "birthday."

The lodge was Savvy's second favorite place, right behind the cabin. It was big and old and rustic and looked like a Swiss chalet.

Upstairs, there was a huge canteen with a cafeteria-style buffet, lots and lots of tables, and a deck with outdoor seating. Downstairs, there were lockers and rooms for the ski clubs to meet.

There was also a lounge with a fireplace big enough to stand up in. And looking out toward the slopes and running the length of the building's front was a restaurant decorated with old wooden skis, carved tables, antler chandeliers, and enormous oil paintings of the lake.

"I feel like Heidi," Ellison whispered as she stared wide-eyed at the thick, carved beams. "I think I might have to yodel."

"Don't!" Lucy exclaimed, giving her a little push. She hated to draw attention.

"Look, you haven't even seen the best part." Savvy pointed out the window as a cute waiter in lederhosen led them to their table.

Outside, a large oval ice rink was lit by white twinkle lights. Skaters slid over the frozen surface. A few in the middle did tricky spins, dancing on the ice, while on the edges, the more teetery skaters clung to the rail. The intermediate skaters circled between.

"Cool," Ellison breathed.

"You mean cold," Lucy corrected her.

"You want to try it after dinner?" Savvy was so excited she practically glided over to the table where her mom and dad were sitting.

Ellison chose a seat next to Savannah and eyed

the rink eagerly, tapping her heels on the cross-bar of her chair, while Lucy slumped forward, picked up her water glass, and mumbled from behind her hair, "I didn't think we were doing anything dangerous until tomorrow."

"It's not that dangerous," came a woman's voice. "Skiing and snowboarding are much riskier."

"Just ignore her," Savannah said with a grin as she got to her feet to give the woman a hug. "Ellison, Lucy, this is my aunt Tilly," she said, making introductions. "She's a ski patrol bigwig on the mountain."

"Well, I wouldn't go that far," Tilly replied, leaning over to hug Savannah's parents before pulling up a chair. "But I do know my way around this bump."

Once everyone was resettled, it was back to perusing the menu.

"The Alpine burgers are amazing," Tilly said, "but the fondue is my favorite, unless you count the lobster." She pointed to the center of the menu just as the waiter reappeared. The girls put their order in and munched on breadsticks while they waited for their sodas. Less than an hour later, three Cokes, three Alpine burgers, and a shared order of sweet potato fries had been demolished.

"Ready for an icy treat?" Savvy asked, gently pulling Lucy to her feet before she could object.

"I wish you were talking about ice cream," Lucy sighed as she followed her friends out into the cold night. Together, Ellison and Savannah gently coaxed Lucy over to the skate rental booth and onto the ice, where she stayed close to the rail and moved with tiny baby steps from one end of the rink to the other.

"I'm doing it!" Lucy squealed as they wobbled farther out. Her tense smile widened into a grin. Savvy and Ellison slowly let go of her arms, and Lucy made it most of the way around the rink before trying to flip her hair out of her face and winding up on her backside. Savvy waited to make sure Lucy was laughing before cracking up herself.

"You're doing great. You should have seen me my first time. I fell so often my pants were soaked after fifteen minutes."

"But weren't you still in diapers?" Lucy said pointedly, dusting herself off and craning to see her backside. "Maybe I should try that. I never thought I'd say it, but I could use some extra padding back here!"

"Yeah, how long *have* you been skating, Savvy?"

Ellison asked. "I think I've only been about ten times. We go at my aunt's house in Idaho whenever we visit. They live by a rink, but it's all inside. It's nothing like this."

Ellison was still rambling and Lucy was inching along when Savvy pushed off toward the center of the rink. It wasn't that she wanted to show off exactly. She was just super-excited and needed to let a little of that energy out. Carving her blades into the ice, she swung in a large arc and then slowed, balancing on one skate. Tipping off with the serrated toe of her left skate, she spun in a tight circle on the right, moving faster and faster as she pulled in her extended leg, arched her back, and tilted her head so she was looking up at the sky.

As she eased her leg back and dug the tip of her skate into the ice to stop, Ellison and Lucy clapped and shouted.

Still dizzy, Savvy met them at the rail.

"You're amazing!" Lucy exclaimed.

Savvy grinned. Her cheeks were cold and her breath was coming in puffs. Ellison clapped her on the back.

"Shredder's good on ice *and* snow," a deeper voice added.

Savvy looked up to see a familiar shaggy head. Eric! She gave him a low five and a quick hug.

"Lucy, Ellison, this is Eric," Savvy said, making introductions.

"Welcome to Powderbowl," Eric greeted her friends. "Are you newbies?"

Ellison grinned widely at him. "Well, I've done a little skiing. But this is Lucy's first time," she offered. "And I think she's feeling —"

"Excited. Totally excited," Lucy insisted, yanking on Ellison's arm before shaking back her hair and smiling.

"Great. Wouldn't expect Savvy to bring along any gapers or butt-draggers," the older boy said with an appreciative nod. "Can't wait to see you on the slopes."

The corners of Eric's brown eyes crinkled into a smile and, without the stocking cap he wore on the slopes, his brown curls flopped over his eyes. "See you tomorrow?" he asked.

"We'll be there!" Savvy waved as Eric glided away.

Slowly, Ellison began to shake her head. Her smile was gone. "Sav, you've totally been holding out on us," she declared, sounding a tiny bit miffed.

25

"I'll say." Lucy nodded.

Savannah had no idea what they were talking about. "What?" she asked.

"He's unbelievably cute!" Ellison exclaimed.

"He is?" Savvy asked. She'd never thought of Eric as cute. But she'd never really thought of Eric that way at all. . . . "Cute?" she said aloud.

"Totally!" her friends replied in unison.

Chapter 3

POW!

"Earth to Savannah, come in, please," a voice echoed across the cabin kitchen. "Um, hello!" Ellison leaned in closer and poked Savvy lightly.

"What?" Savannah pulled her eyes away from the kitchen window. Snow had fallen all night, frosting everything with a thick, fluffy layer of white, and the day had dawned sunny and bright. Bluebird for sure. In her head, Savvy was already making her milk run — the first run of the day — and cutting fresh lines in the pow.

"Pass the syrup," Ellison said with a smirk. "My pancakes are thirsty."

Savannah grinned and handed the jug of Vermont Grade A to her friend. "Sorry," she mumbled. "I was just trying to figure out what we should do — ski or board," she explained as she forked up a large bite of pancake. Skiing was cool, especially going off piste — getting away from the crowds. But Lucy probably wouldn't be ready for that for a while, and boarding was Savvy's new obsession. There were so many fun tricks to do!

"I vote for snowboarding," Ellison said. "I think those snowboard boots are adorable! And they don't make you walk funny like ski boots." She had braided her hair into two long plaits and looped them up with rubber bands. The loops bounced when she talked, making her look extra animated.

Lucy put down her fork, a look of mild panic crossing her face. "Snowboarding? On the first day? Maybe I can just hang out in the lodge. . . . You know, get some visual tips."

"What happened to all that excitement you were telling Eric about last night?" Savvy teased before picking up her glass of juice and taking a swig.

"I *am* excited," Lucy gulped. "It's just —"

"It will be fine, I promise," Savvy said earnestly. "We'll take it slow — no black diamonds until tomorrow."

Lucy's eyes widened in horror. Savvy'd given her a trail guide with the rating symbols listed so she knew black diamonds were out of her league. Waaaay out of her league.

"I'm kidding!" Savannah insisted. "We'll stick to the green circles until you say so. And starting the week with boarding will give you plenty of time to get used to it."

"And you won't ditch me?" Lucy wanted to know.

Savannah and Ellison raised their hands and linked pinkies in the friendship promise the trio had made up when they were eight. "And we won't ditch you!" they vowed.

A nervous smile spread across Lucy's face as she stood up and carried her dishes to the sink. Savannah and Ellison were right on her heels.

"Dad, we're ready to go!" Savannah shouted at the top of her lungs.

"Savvy, your dad's upstairs, not on the mountain," Ellison teased. "Don't go starting any avalanches."

"Avalanches?" Lucy echoed.

"I was *kidding*, Lu," Ellison reassured her, slinging an arm around her friend's shoulders. "Totally, completely kidding."

"Be right down," Mr. Heglund called.

The girls quickly slathered their faces with

SPF 45, donned their bibs and ski jackets, and pulled on hats and gloves.

"Don't forget your goggles," Savannah warned. "It's going to be superbright out there."

Minutes later, they were all piled into the car and heading up to Powderbowl. The resort was bustling with people in snow gear buying lift tickets, carrying skis and boards, and — the lucky ducks — already loading onto chairlifts. Savannah was so excited it was hard for her not to leap out of the car before it came to a stop.

"Hold up there, missy," her dad said, eyeing her hand on the door handle. Finally, her father pulled into the drop-off area. "*Now* you can get out," he said, but the girls were already unloading.

"Thanks, Dad!" Savannah called as she walked around to the back of the wagon. Since Savvy's aunt Tilly worked on the mountain, Savannah's parents were pretty relaxed about leaving her to do runs all day without them. As long as she was home by dinner, everything was cool.

"Let's stop by the sport shop before we get your boards," Savvy suggested as she pulled hers out of the back of the car. "There's someone else I want you to meet."

She led her friends into a smallish shop packed with all kinds of snow gear — hats, gloves, goggles, glasses, jackets, bibs, helmets, skis, poles, boards, boots — you name it.

"Savannah, luv," greeted a tall, balding man working the register. "You've returned!"

"Yup," Savannah replied with an elated smile. "And for the whole week!" She turned to her two best friends. "I want you to meet my friends, Ellison and Lucy. Guys, this is Hector."

Hector reached across the wooden counter and shook hands with each of the girls. "Any mate of Savannah's is a mate of mine," he declared. "You girls need anything before you head up the mountain today? Sunscreen? Lip balm?"

"We're all slathered up, thanks," Ellison reported.

Savannah eyed the light green Burton hanging on the wall behind Hector. "Not unless you're sending the board of my dreams out for demos," she said with a wishful sigh. "No offense," she added in a whisper to her current board.

"Sorry, luv," Hector replied sympathetically. "No can do. But she is a beaut, that's for sure."

Savannah slipped behind the counter and ran a hand along the varnished board.

"So this is it, huh?" Lucy asked.

"At last we meet the infamous board," Ellison added. "We've been hearing about it all winter."

"Savannah knows a good design when she sees one," Hector noted. "She picked that one out of a whole shop full. It's kind of amazing she's still here, actually — the board, not Savvy," Hector added with a sly smile. "You'd have to pry Savannah here off the mountain."

"Didn't I tell you? I put my special invisibility hex on her," Savvy joked. "Seriously, she's waiting until I can seal the deal. I've saved up a hundred and sixty dollars already. Only one more hundred to go — she'll be mine by the end of the season."

"And then you'll *really* be something on the slopes," Hector said, his eyes twinkling.

The girls waved good-bye to Hector and headed across the hall to the rental shop to get Lucy and Ellison outfitted. Inside, there were racks and racks of skis, boots, and boards in all colors and sizes, and a whole pack of high school and college-age ski buffs fitting everybody out. The girls filled in some forms on clipboards, then tried on a couple of pairs of snowboard boots to get a good fit while the ski-shop folks selected their boards. A quick lesson in bindings and they were good to go.

"Now we're set!" Savannah chortled as the girls lugged their gear out to the bottom of the beginner's run. Savannah quickly strapped her left foot onto her board and helped her friends do the same, making sure the straps were tight. "You leave the other foot loose until we get to the top," she explained, gesturing to the gorgeous mountain behind her. "And we're on our way up there right now!"

She and Ellison headed over to the lift. Savvy was so anxious she didn't notice that Lucy wasn't following them. "Lu, come on!" she called when she finally realized the trio had become a duo.

Lucy held back her floppy bangs with one hand and stared wide-eyed at the sky chair. But she didn't budge.

Savannah quickly returned to her friend's side.

"I can't!" Lucy whispered plaintively.

"We just have to get on the chair, Lu," Savannah said. "It's easy."

Chair after chair came down the hill empty, whirled around the big gear at the bottom to change direction, and swooped forward to pick up riders from the lift line without slowing down.

"It doesn't look easy," Lucy replied.

Just then a group of Ski Wees — little kids taking lessons — scurried to the front of the line and slid onto the seat of the chairlift. They didn't even have an adult riding with them. One of the smallest kids actually had to jump up a little to get his rump on the chair, which he did like it was nothing at all.

"See that? If those little dudes can do it, so can you," Savannah insisted. "And remember, you can't come down if you don't go up."

Biting her lip, Lucy dragged her snowboard to the end of the lift line. "Can't go down if you don't go up," she whispered to herself.

Savannah gave the operator a look to let him know Lucy was new at this. The liftie gave a nod and hit a button that slowed everything down.

"Ready? Sit now!" Savvy instructed.

Lucy sat, the chair swung back slightly, then forward. Two seconds later, the three girls were on their way up the mountain.

"Hey, that *was* pretty easy," Lucy admitted as the chair rose higher into the air.

Below them, a snowboarder carefully weaved his way down the wide hill. Savvy pointed at him. "This hill is great for beginners," Savannah explained. "It's nice and wide, and not too steep. No moguls." She gave her friends quick instructions on how to get off the chair — a review course for Ellison — and they all made it to the bottom of the little incline at the end of the lift without incident. Then they strapped their second boots onto their bindings and started to make their way s-l-o-w-l-y down the hill.

"Keep your knees a little bent, and most of your weight on your front foot," Savannah advised as she carved an easy turn. "Use your arms for balance. If you're going to fall, fall backward."

Ahead of them, Ellison was already carving her own turns, sending a spray of snow down the mountain. She was a natural.

Lucy slid ahead of Savvy into the shadow of a tree, skidded down an icy patch of snow and landed on her butt with an "oof."

Savannah quickly slid in front to offer a hand. She searched her friend's face to gauge her reaction. She wanted boarding to be fun for Lucy, not scary. Lucy's face was a blank mask for a second, and then she grinned up at her friend. "That didn't really hurt," she said. "And I got one thing right. I fell back!" Lucy laughed. She got to her feet and steadied herself without help before continuing down the hill at a snail's pace. "I have a feeling I might be spending a lot of time on my butt," she yelled as she inched along.

Savannah watched her negotiate a wobbly turn, staying upright. "Go, Lucy!" she cheered.

Then from out of nowhere, a group of Ski Wees whizzed past. Their heavy-jacketed arms stuck out at their sides, and their instructor struggled to keep up. They passed Lucy on both sides, surprising her. The poor girl helicoptered — her arms spinning in circles — for almost a full minute before going over again.

Savvy stifled a laugh behind her glove until she heard Lucy laughing at herself.

By the time they got to the bottom of the run, Lucy had snow all over her backside and in her hair. But her eyes were sparkling, and she didn't hesitate for a second before stepping back into the line. "Come on!" she called to her friends. "The mountain won't wait forever!"

The girls boarded all morning, taking a lunch break in the lodge at midday. With a plate of chicken fingers and a giant tower of fries between them, they chatted excitedly.

"Did you see that last spill I took?" Ellison asked. "I can still feel the snow melting down my back." She shivered.

"Oh, you should talk," Lucy piped up. "Did you catch *my* last fall? My stuff went flying! It was a total yard sale."

Savvy slapped a hand over her mouth to keep from spewing ketchup when she laughed. Lucy was picking up the lingo fast!

Ellison choked on her fries. "Yard sale!" she repeated. "Good one."

Out of the corner of her eye, Savannah watched a teenager chase a little kid in a snowsuit across the cafeteria. The older girl was moving fast, but the tyke was moving even faster.

"Those little kids are really something," Lucy said, following Savannah's gaze. "I mean, they're fearless out there!"

"They're also closer to the ground," Ellison pointed out. "When they wipe out they don't have far to fall."

The girls chuckled over this as they polished off the heap of fries.

"Delicious," Savvy said. The girls dropped the garbage into the bin and headed over to the giant stone fireplace to warm up.

After a few minutes, Savannah pulled her gloves on. "Ready for a few more runs?" she asked.

"Ready!" her friends chorused.

Outside, the sun was already beginning to drop in the sky, but there wasn't a cloud in sight as they got onto the lift. The cold air was bracing and Savvy felt a wave of happiness as she glided up the mountain between her two best friends. Ski-week was off to an amazing start!

"Let's try Culver's Snow Park," Ellison suggested, pointing as they passed the all-terrain run off to the left. "It's not as crowded as it was this morning."

"Fine with me," Lucy agreed, ". . . as long as I don't have to go over any of those crazy-looking jumps."

Savannah nodded. "They're not as crazy as they look, but you're off the hook. The half-pipe is more fun than the jumps, anyway."

"I'll leave that to you," Lucy vowed. "I'll stick close to my new best friend . . . the snow. In case you haven't noticed, we've completely bonded."

The girls got off the lift like pros, shoved their second boots into the clamps, and headed down the run toward Culver's. At the top of the half-pipe, Savvy sent out an arcing spray of snow as she stopped to wait for her friends. On the other side of the pipe, Eric was watching a few of his students try out some new tricks. He had his jacket off and wore layered T-shirts and a bandanna tied on his head. Savvy waved, and Eric raised his hand in salute. "Shredder!" he called.

A little tingle of excitement ran through Savvy's veins. This was the perfect chance to live up to the words of praise Eric had spoken the night before — a chance to show her friends just how good she could be on the snow. She looked around to make sure the coast was clear and Eric was watching, then threw her friends a grin.

"Check it," she said. Leaning forward just enough, she launched herself into the half-pipe. Her board dropped in fast, gliding down the entry ramp and sailing up toward the platform. She got ready to pull one of her fave tricks, a backside 360. Bending her knees to pick up speed, she started the climb. Seconds later, she approached the lip, wind whistled in her ears, and she was ready for takeoff. With expert ease, Savvy launched herself into the air and turned the board and her body together, rotating in midair. She came around easily with height to spare. She was going big!

Still airborne, a thought flashed through Savvy's adrenaline-charged brain: *I could pull a 720!* Her height and her speed were enough to take her around in a second circle. Rushing, she started a second rotation, but in a heartbeat she knew she'd misjudged. She'd gotten greedy. In a flash, everything went wrong.

The ground came up too fast, the board came down too quickly, and Savannah landed hard with her weight on her awkwardly positioned left leg. She heard a sickening crunch — like car wheels on gravel — and everything went black.

Chapter 4

The Breaks

Savvy felt herself being jostled before she even opened her eyes. A dull pain in her ankle reminded her of the fall, and her eyes flew open. Where was she?

"Savvy, are you all right?" Aunt Tilly was sitting at her feet in the ski-patrol toboggan, looking anxious.

"Aunt Tilly," Savvy muttered. And that was all. She closed her eyes again and tried to ignore the dizziness enveloping her. The toboggan was lashed to the back of a snowmobile traveling down the hill pretty fast. And her ankle was throbbing.

"Savvy, are you okay?" her aunt repeated.

"I think so," Savvy replied, biting her lip. Talking made her head spin even faster.

"We're taking you to the hospital," her aunt said. "Eric said your fall was pretty bad, and we need to take a look at that ankle ASAP."

The memory of the fall flooded Savannah's brain and she turned her face to the side to hide her tears. It was so stupid to show off in front of Eric and her friends. She'd made a fool of herself. And now she was on her way to the hospital!

An ambulance was already waiting in the parking lot and, as Savvy was transferred from the toboggan to a gurney and loaded inside, her aunt called her parents. "She'll be fine," Savvy heard Aunt Tilly say. Her stomach lurched and her head swam. She hoped her aunt was right.

By the time she was being wheeled into the emergency room at Tahoe Forest Hospital, her friends and her parents were already in the waiting room.

"Oh, Savannah," her mother said, looking worried and reproachful at the same time. Savvy could tell by the look in her mom's eyes that she wished her daughter would be more careful, less impulsive, and, for goodness' sake, look before she leaped! Savvy had heard it before. And for once, Savvy wished she had listened.

"Savannah!" Ellison cried, leaping out of her chair. "Are you all right? That fall looked just awful. Awful!" Her brown eyes were full of concern. "I was sure you'd have a concussion. I mean —"

"I think she's okay, El," Lucy said, whacking her talkative friend on the arm and giving her a look at the same time. "And she knows all about the fall — she was there, remember?"

Ellison's hand flew to her mouth in embarrassment. "Oh, of course," she said.

"I'm okay guys, really," Savannah assured them, despite the fact that she felt shaky all over and her ankle was absolutely killing her.

"You'll be fine, but we need to get you through triage," her aunt said, "so a doctor can see you."

"You guys don't have to stay here," Savannah told her friends, feeling guilty that her recklessness had brought them to the hospital on their first day out.

"We're here, and we're staying," Lucy said as Ellison nodded emphatically.

Savannah felt a little wave of relief as her mom wheeled her over to the check-in nurse. She wanted her friends to stay, even if they were out in the waiting room.

Savvy's aunt gave the nurse a whole bunch of information, and they took her temperature and blood pressure, then gave her an ice pack for her ankle. "You're lucky it's slow today," the nurse said. "Yesterday it was packed, and the wait to see a doctor was four hours."

"And today?" Savannah ventured.

"Today, I practically have a doctor waiting for *you*," the nurse replied with a smile.

"I'd better get back to the mountain," Aunt Tilly said when they'd made it through triage. "Call me as soon as you know anything."

"We will. Thanks, Tilly." Savannah's dad gave his sister a hug. "So glad you were there."

Savvy and her parents were escorted through triage, then to a "room" with a curtain for walls. Savannah fanned a little flame of hope. Maybe her ankle wasn't actually broken — maybe that chrunching sound she'd heard was just her board scraping the icy snow. If she only had a sprain she might be able to —

The curtain was pushed aside and a man with graying hair and a blue lab coat appeared. "Hi, I'm Dr. Marshall," he said slowly. "And you must be Savannah the super snowboard girl." He looked up from his chart and smiled. "Let's take a look at that ankle."

Savannah winced as Dr. Marshall reached down, pulled back the ice pack, and gently lifted her calf and ankle higher for a better look. "It's not too swollen, which is good," he said as he began to press lightly in a variety of places.

"Ouch!" Savannah yelped when he got to the top of her ankle bone.

"Sorry," the doctor said. "Comes with the territory." He put the ice back on her ankle and secured it with a stretchy ACE bandage, then stood up and made some notes on Savannah's chart. "I'm going to order some X-rays so we can see what's going on in there."

Savannah groaned inwardly. That did not sound good.

"I'll try to get you and your friends out of here as soon as I can," he half whispered to Savannah. "But taking care of that ankle comes first."

Savvy laid her head back on her wheelchair with a sigh. She couldn't really argue with that, no matter how badly she wanted to.

By the time the results of her X-rays came back — more than two hours later — Savannah's aunt had called three times. Savannah was bored, bored, bored, and waited anxiously for Dr. Marshall to give her the word.

"I'm afraid you've got a fracture in your ankle bone." He pointed to a dark line on the giant black-and-white negatives hanging on the viewing box on the wall. "We need to put you in a cast."

This time Savvy groaned aloud. A cast? How was she going to board and ski and skate and play in a cast?! She finally had to admit that her hope of a simple sprain had been pretty far-fetched.

Another hour later, Savannah and her new cast hobbled on crutches into the waiting room.

"A cast!" Ellison said, letting out a breath. "Oh, Savannah."

"Tell me about it," Savvy grumbled in agreement. "I broke my ankle."

"Let's look on the bright side," Lucy said. "We're still in Tahoe — together — and Savvy's birthday is right around the corner. It's not all bad!"

Right, Savannah thought as she made her way toward the door, accidentally whacking the frame as she passed through. Crutches were a lot more awkward than ski poles.

Outside, her dad pulled the car around so Savvy would not have to negotiate the slushy parking lot. As they were climbing inside the station wagon, Savannah saw a familiar-looking little boy being wheeled into the hospital. His face was red and blotchy, and he was sobbing uncontrollably. She couldn't be sure, but he

looked like one of the tykes that had helped con-
vince Lucy to get onto the chairlift earlier that day.
Except now his happy-go-lucky demeanor had been
transformed into misery. He'd caught a bad break,
and Savvy knew just how he felt.

Everyone worked extra hard to cheer Savvy up
that evening. With giant mugs of cocoa and extra
marshmallows, the girls settled in for a game of
Scrabble back at the cabin.

"Don't worry, Savannah," Lucy said as she laid
S-N-O-W-Y down on the board. "We can just hang
out in the cabin together. There are lots of games
to play, and we can —"

"No," Savannah said firmly as she gazed at the
feathery flakes that were beginning to fall outside.
She felt grateful to her friends for their willingness
to hang out with her. But she had brought them
up here for some fun in the snow, and they had
already spent an entire afternoon in a hospital
waiting room — all because of her foolish attempt
to show off. "I promised you guys a great week in
the snow, and I want you to have it . . . even if I
can't have it with you."

Chapter 5

Après Ski

When Savannah awoke the next morning, snow was still falling softly to the ground. But close to the horizon the sun was starting to break through the clouds — perfect conditions again. Savannah felt a surge of excitement, then remembered her broken ankle. The mountain beckoned, but she was trapped inside a fitted piece of fiberglass. The cast sank her mood so quickly it might as well have been a pair of cement galoshes.

"Ready for breakfast?" Lucy called from the doorway. "We made scrambled eggs and bacon."

"Sure," Savannah replied, realizing in an instant that she was not at all hungry. "I'll be right down." She pulled on a pair of sweats — the only thing she could find that fit over her cast — and her Powderbowl shirt. Then she hobbled down the stairs to the kitchen, where her friends were busily getting everything ready.

"Step right up," Ellison said, pulling out a chair for her friend.

Savannah smiled and all three girls sat down at the table. "Looks delicious."

"We know you told us you want us to go skiing and boarding without you," Lucy said as she buttered a piece of toast. "But we'd rather hang out with you today."

Savvy felt a wave of relief as she took a bite of cheesy eggs. But before she'd even swallowed she was hit by a second wave — of guilt. Just a few feet away on the other side of the glass was a fresh layer of powdery snow, ready and waiting for her friends. It wouldn't be fair to saddle them with her stupid mistake. "That's totally sweet of both of you," she said. "Really. But I'm not feeling so hot today. I'm not even up for UNO. I think I'll just hang out in the lodge and read. You two should go boarding. You were really getting the hang of it, and the snow will be amazing."

Ellison and Lucy looked at each other across the table for a very long moment. "Only if we can have lunch with you," Lucy finally said.

"Great," Savvy faked a winning smile. "Now let's get out to that shuttle."

After outfitting the bare toes that stuck out of the end of her cast with a stocking cap, Savvy discovered that walking on crutches was waaay harder than skiing, boarding, or skating — especially on snow. It took Savannah a long time to make it out to the shuttle stop — even with her friends flanking her in case she started to fall.

"Just a little farther," Lucy encouraged as the bus pulled up.

The three girls climbed on and found a seat near the front.

"Maybe you guys should get me a sled," Savvy tried to joke. She pictured herself being dragged along behind her friends like dead weight. "And a dog team."

Lucy smiled sympathetically, but Ellison was staring out the window. "The snow really does look perfect," she noted. "I wonder what part of the mountain Eric is going to take me on."

"Eric?" Savannah echoed, unable to keep the surprise out of her voice. She felt a flash of annoyance.

"Yeah, he came by the hospital and offered to give me a couple of tips today," she said, looking sheepish. "Since you can't. I was going to cancel, but . . ."

"She really needs it," Lucy put in with a laugh.

"Like you don't!" Ellison replied.

"Hey, anyone could use a lesson from Eric," Savvy said, settling the quarrel as the shuttle pulled up outside the lodge. "He's the best." Hadn't he taught her? He'd probably offered to help her friend as a favor. But as Savvy got to her feet she found herself wishing he hadn't.

Luckily, the Powderbowl shuttle stop had been cleared, so it wasn't too difficult for Savannah to make her way into the lodge. Her friends got her settled in front of the giant river-rock fireplace with a comfy chair, a footstool, and as many pillows as they could scrounge up.

"You sure you'll be okay?" Ellison asked, biting her lip.

No! Savannah wanted to scream. "Of course," she replied. "Now get out there and learn some great stuff."

"We'll be back at twelve o'clock sharp for lunch." Lucy tapped her watch before slipping on her soft, gray gloves.

"Right," Savannah agreed. "I'll be here." Where else could she possibly be?

As her friends turned to leave the lodge, a lump rose in Savannah's throat. She watched them head out to the ski rack, unlock their equipment, and strap it on. A few minutes later they were hopping onto the triple chair bound for the top, leaving a seat open in the middle. *My seat!* Savannah thought as she watched her friends move away from her, getting smaller and smaller as they were carried up the mountain.

Tearing her gaze away from the slopes, Savannah stared at the cast propped up on the pillows — her cast. Her stupid, annoying, won't-let-her-do-anything cast. Lifting her leg a few inches above the pillow, she let the awkward extra-large foot drop back to the cushion, and regretted it. Waves of pain rippled up her leg.

With a giant you-did-this-to-yourself sigh, Savvy picked up her book and started to read. She willed the book to lure her in and make her forget where she was and what she was missing. But the story was dull and dreary, and the minutes dragged so, so slowly. It seemed to Savannah that lunchtime would never come.

At 11:58, she spotted her friends coming down the hill. They skidded to a stop outside the lodge and unstrapped their equipment. Then they burst through the lodge door, their cheeks rosy and their smiles bright.

"How was your morning?" Lucy asked, unzipping her jacket and plopping herself down next to Savannah.

"I'm starved!" Ellison bubbled as she pulled off her colorful fleece hat and shook snow all over. "What will it be today, Savvy? Chicken fingers or clam chowder? Both come with fries and a soda, of course."

"I think I'll have a salad," Savannah replied, realizing that she didn't feel like a lot of heavy food. She hadn't been burning much energy turning pages, and the eggs from breakfast still felt like a scrambled lump in her stomach.

"Suit yourself," Ellison replied. "I'm going for the chicken and extra fries. All that boarding really works up an appetite."

And all this lying around really . . . makes me bored, Savannah thought. But she didn't say it out loud. She knew her friend wasn't trying to be mean, and she didn't want to make her feel bad.

"I'm so glad you guys are having fun," Savvy said, forcing a smile. "It looks sick out there. You'll have to fill me in on all the snowy details."

"It is sooo perfect," Ellison said. "And you were totally right about Eric. Not only is he adorable, he's an awesome teacher. I'm already carving tighter turns!"

"And check it out. I'm practically dry!" Lucy added, turning and patting her backside. "Not so many butt-plants today . . . I mean, I still went over. Don't get me wrong. But I can just sort of biff, and then pop right back up. I'm not making bathtubs anymore."

Savvy had to laugh. In just two days, Lucy was starting to sound like a serious powder hound! Still, behind the laugh, Savannah felt a pang of envy, and sadness.

Her friends didn't need her to become experts on the slopes. And worse, they didn't even miss her — they were having too much fun together, and with Eric! She did her best to make conversation and seem upbeat during lunch, but as soon as her friends headed back out to the mountain, Savannah caved in on herself. Biting her lip, she tried not to cry as she watched her friends laugh together while they strapped on their boards. It was no use — she felt totally, completely bummed out. And, she suddenly realized, she was also totally, completely done watching skiers and boarders — her two best friends among them — have the time of their lives on the perfect snowy slopes.

Chapter 6

All Downhill

When the sun sent a golden shaft of light into the cabin dorm early the next morning, Savannah rolled over and pulled her pillow over her head to shut it out. She must have gone back to sleep, because the next thing she knew the whole room was brightly lit, her hair was plastered to her cheek with sweat, and her friends' beds were empty.

With a thunk, she lowered her cast to the floor and hobbled down to breakfast. She figured Lucy and Ellison had probably started eating without her, but when she got to the kitchen she saw that they weren't even there.

"Morning, sweetie!" Savvy's mom chirped. She was sitting at the table reading the paper and sipping coffee.

"Morning," Savvy mumbled, looking around in a daze. "Where are Lucy and Ellison?" she finally asked. The bathroom was too small for both of them to squeeze into at once and the living room was empty. "And Dad?" she added.

"Eric offered the girls a free ski lesson this morning, but only if they could get there before his regular sessions started. Your dad drove them to the lodge." Savvy could feel her mom studying her face for a reaction. Savvy did her best not to let her "left-out fever" show.

"Hope he doesn't forget about the no-singing rule," Savvy joked feebly.

"At least the ride's short," her mom offered, passing Savvy a box of cereal. "I thought you and I could stay here today, do some reading, maybe bake cookies before we meet the girls for lunch."

Savvy knew her mom was trying to cheer her up, but the last thing she wanted was to see the sympathetic look on her face . . . all day. It only made her feel worse.

"I was thinking about going back to the lodge to wait." Savvy shrugged before tossing a couple of dry flakes in her mouth and filling her bowl. She tried to rustle up some enthusiasm — and an appetite — for cold cereal and another boring day in the lodge. It wasn't easy.

Savvy's mom looked concerned. "If you're sure," she said slowly. "Lucy and Ellison said they wanted to have lunch with you. And I guess it would be nice to go back out with your dad. We found a great trail yesterday. I have to admit this snowshoeing thing is better than I thought. Who knew slowing down could be so much fun?"

Not me, thought Savannah. Slowing down was seriously bumming her out. With a resigned sigh, she realized chicken fingers were probably going to be the highlight of her day.

Propping her cast on a lodge stool and settling into the most comfortable chair she could find, Savannah pulled three fresh paperbacks from her pack. She'd raided Lucy's stash — the girl had brought about ten different books — and was hoping that one of them would be her ticket out of here, at least in her mind. She had just cracked the first one, a mystery, when out of the corner of her eye she spotted a low-flying pink parka hurtling right toward her ankle, squealing.

In one quick movement Savannah dropped her book and threw out her arm to protect her injured leg. The padded projectile came to a halt, but the squealing continued.

"Take it easy," Savvy soothed, though her own heart was beating a million pumps a second. "Where are you in there, anyway?" The well-wrapped little person was completely hidden inside a hat, scarf, hood, rose-colored coat, and matching puffy pants. Locating the end of the fuzzy, striped scarf, Savvy started to unwrap.

After peeling off a few layers, the squealing turned to a muffled squeak. "Are you okay?" Savvy asked. Maybe the kid was suffocating. She pulled up the knit hat that had slumped down to cover most of the girl's face and discovered a very flushed blond preschooler with a panicked look in her eyes.

"Is it gone?" the girl asked. The second her mittens were off, she grabbed Savannah's hand and clung to it tightly. "Is it gone?" she repeated, looking around nervously.

"Is what gone?" Savvy started to scan the area. The lodge had the mellow bustle of mid-morning, but that was all.

"The monster cat," the girl said. She shivered in spite of her generously layered fleece.

"The what?" Savvy asked, confused.

"The giant monster cat," the girl repeated. "The one that goes up and down the mountain! The noisy growly one!" The poor kid's voice was almost a wail.

"You mean the snowcat? The groomers?" Savvy couldn't help but smile. When she was small she was terrified of the huge tractorlike snow-grooming machines, too. Now she just hated the little hard packs of icy snow they sometimes left behind, the chunks Eric called "death cookies." "Oh, those cats aren't allowed inside," she explained calmly.

The girl took a deep breath and loosened her grip on Savvy's hand. "They're not?"

"No. This is a cat-free zone. Not only is it against the rules, they don't fit through the door. We're totally safe here. And you know what else?"

The girl shook her head.

"They're actually really friendly," Savvy whispered.

The girl's mouth dropped open.

"Really. They work for Frosty."

"The snowman?" the girl asked. Her eyes were wide with wonder.

"The one and only." Savannah gave a serious nod before asking the girl her name.

"Gretchen," she answered.

"Nice to meet you, Gretchen. I'm Savvy. So, uh, where are you supposed to be?" she asked. Out of the corner of her eye she had been watching for a parent or adult to show up and claim the kid, but the lodge was practically deserted. Savvy was about to suggest they head for the lost and found when a panic-stricken teenager came running into the lodge's main room. The girl was tall, older than Savannah, and completely out of breath. Spotting Gretchen, she looked visibly relieved and hurried over.

"Oh, good," she panted. "You've got her. Last time she ran all the way down to the rental shop."

"I'm fast." Gretchen nodded.

"I'm Carmen." The teenager stuck out her hand and Savvy shook it with her left, since Gretchen still had a hold of her right.

"Savannah."

"She knows Frosty," Gretchen informed the older girl.

"Cool," Carmen said, her breath slowing to a normal rate. "But we've gotta get back. I left five more kids in the room."

Savvy looked baffled.

"Ski Wees," Carmen explained. "Their parents drop them off in the morning so they can get some slope time on their own. They all get lessons at some point during the day, but also spend a lot of time in the lodge with me. And only me, since the other girl they hired didn't bother to show up this week." Carmen tugged on Gretchen's other hand. "Not that you asked." She smiled at Savvy, shaking her head. "Guess I'm a little frazzled. Let's go, kid." Carmen tugged again on Gretchen's hand, but Gretchen wouldn't let go of Savvy.

"How about I walk you back?" Savvy offered. "Or limp you back," she corrected, rolling her eyes at her bum leg and gathering her crutches.

"Oh, could you? That would be so great." Carmen smiled gratefully at Savannah and scooped up Gretchen's shed layers along with Savvy's bag of books. "Who knows what they're up to in there?" She nodded toward a door at the end of the long hall. Soft blocks were flying out of it, and Savvy could hear both shrieks of delight and other not-so-happy cries coming from inside. It sounded like chaos.

If it *sounded* like chaos, it *looked* like utter mayhem. Gretchen pulled Savvy inside the tot room proudly, like she was some sort of giant-sized teddy she'd brought for show-and-tell, and Savvy tried not to laugh out loud. The kids had made a towering pile in the middle of the room with everything they could find, starting with chairs and ending with jackets. Now they were trying to knock it over with whatever was left — water bottles, lunch boxes, books — anything that wasn't tied down. Only one kid sat quietly in a corner with his head on his knees. Savvy guessed maybe he was pouting.

"Okay, okay!" Carmen called to get everyone's attention. "It's cleanup time. I want everyone to put away four things. I'll go first." Carmen hung several coats on hooks while Savvy sank into a chair. The kids started grabbing stuff, too, and for a minute it was almost sane. Then a girl with braids and a boy with curls both tried to put away the same block and it was pandemonium all over again.

Before she could think about what she was doing, Savvy held up her hand and made an announcement. "Everyone who has put away four things can come sit with me for a story."

Three kids shuffled over and sat in front of Savvy's chair with their legs crossed. Gretchen handed Savvy a book, *The Mitten*, and cuddled up next to her uninjured leg.

Before Savvy had gotten through three pages, everyone was sitting quietly, listening. Even the kid in the corner turned a little so he could hear.

When the story ended, Carmen put her hand on Savvy's shoulder. "Don't ever leave me," she joked, batting her eyelashes.

Savvy laughed. "Well, it's not like I have some-where to go," she said, nodding down at her cast. "I'm not going to be strapping onto my board any-time soon, that's for sure."

"Wait, you mean that?" Carmen looked stunned. "Are you saying you can stay and help?" The hope in her eyes was hard to resist.

"Sure." Savannah shrugged, looking around the brightly painted room and the kids bouncing around it like pinballs. She didn't have tons of babysitting experience, but it seemed simple enough. Besides, hanging with the Ski Wees beat sitting around feeling sorry for herself.

The morning passed incredibly quickly. After stories, some of the kids had lessons, and getting them dressed was no small affair. By the time they were gone, there was just enough time for a game of Duck, Duck, Goose! before the kids started clam-oring for food.

At the long table at the side of the room, Carmen and Savvy unpacked insulated coolers of chocolate milk, string cheese, fruit, and sand-wiches. They swabbed spills, wiped chins, and even got a couple of the younger kids down for a rest on blankets in the reading corner. By the time she checked her watch it was four o'clock and parents were arriving to collect their kids. Savvy hugged Gretchen, who excitedly announced to her dad that her newest friend knew Frosty.

"The snowman? Really?" he asked.

Gretchen's head bobbed up and down.

"Is he as cheerful as he seems?" her dad wanted to know.

Savannah laughed. "Absolutely."

Gretchen showed her dad the drawing she had done while they collected her clothes.

"Thanks for your help," Gretchen's dad said, handing Savannah a few bills for a tip. A couple of other parents did the same before they left. Savvy shoved the money in her pockets until the last kid had gone, then offered it to Carmen.

"Here," she said, holding out the bills.

Carmen pulled out her own handful of money. "We split tips fifty-fifty," she explained, counting out twenty dollars for Savvy. "And if you want to come back for the rest of the week, I can find out what the lodge will pay you. You'll probably have to fill out a bunch of forms."

Savvy blinked at the bills in her hand. She hadn't really been thinking of this as a real job.

"So . . . can you be here at nine thirty tomorrow?"

The light green Burton board in the ski shop — *her* light green Burton board — flashed in

Savannah's mind. She was already twenty dollars closer to owning it, and one step closer to salvaging her derailed ski week. Thanks to her day with the Ski Wees, things were looking up.

"I'll be here," Savvy agreed with a grin.

Chapter 7

Cut and Paste

"Where were you at lunch?" Ellison demanded the second that Savvy was aboard the shuttle.

"Yeah, we missed you," Lucy said. She sounded less peevish than Ellison and offered to hold Savannah's crutches so she could maneuver into a seat. "We came in late for a bowl of chili and couldn't find you anywhere."

"And Lucy wouldn't eat chicken fingers with me," Ellison groused.

Savannah felt a pang of guilt. She had completely forgotten about having lunch with her friends! "Sorry, guys," she said. "Something came up."

"Something came up?" Ellison echoed.

"I know. Crazy, right? You aren't going to believe

this, but . . . I got a job," Savvy said happily. It felt really good to have something interesting to say about *her* day.

"You did what?" Ellison asked, floored. Lucy was speechless.

And when Savannah explained how she spent her afternoon, and how she planned to spend the next several . . . well, both of her friends just sat there gaping.

"Why?" Ellison finally asked. Savvy could not count all the times Ellison had complained that her younger siblings made her nuts. If it were up to Ellison all kids under six would be caged.

"Actually, the kids are kind of cute." Savvy shrugged. "And they're funny, too." She neglected to mention that having Gretchen worship her like some sort of superhero just because she could reach a high shelf was not a bad perk. "So long as they don't drool, need diaper changing, or wipe snot on me . . . they're pretty cool."

"Wait. You changed *diapers*?" Lucy's eyes were popping as they got off the bus.

"No. No. Don't panic," Savvy clarified. "They are all potty trained. The worst we have to do is wipe noses."

Ellison breathed a sigh of relief. "Well, that's

good. 'Cause if you'd started changing diapers for fun, it would have meant another day in the hospital."

"Really? Why?" Savvy asked, not getting it.

"'Cause we would've had to take you in for head X-rays."

At dinner, Savvy's parents were just as surprised to hear her news as her friends had been.

"Well, that's a happy happenstance," her dad said. "It's got to feel good to be filling your days and earning a little money at the same time."

Savannah nodded as she and her friends cleared the table and started in on the dishes. When they were done, they all settled onto the couches in the living room.

"Carmen is supercool," Savannah said as Lucy painted Savvy's toenails a bright purple. "I can't wait for you guys to meet her. Maybe tomorrow at lunch?"

"Don't move," Lucy scolded. She held Savannah's plaster-wrapped foot on her lap. "I almost got nail polish all over your sweats." She dabbed polish on Savvy's exposed baby toe.

"I don't know about tomorrow. I was going to take Lucy to the Outpost for lunch now that she's graduated to blue square runs." Ellison beamed.

"You should see her go, Sav. Lucy's a total natural. Who would've thought?"

Savannah's smile faded. *She* would have thought. But she'd also thought she would be the one teaching Lucy how to shred, not Ellison. And she thought she would be with them, all three of them together, celebrating at the Outpost — the lunch spot at the top of the hill — after their first blue square run.

"I'd love to wear it. But are you really sure you don't mind?" Ellison asked for a second time. She held Savvy's turquoise-and-white ski jacket up under her chin and turned slightly, admiring herself in the big mirror in the lodge.

"Nah. Take it. It's not like I need a jacket where I'm headed," Savannah said, looking down the hall. She watched a couple blow kisses to their little one and head out the door. The Ski Wees were gathering. She had to go.

"Do you guys have a second to come meet the kids and Carmen?" Savvy asked. "I bet most of them will be there by now."

"Oh, but Eric's waiting." Lucy cringed. "We told him —"

"We'll come by before four," Ellison reassured her. "We'll meet everybody then, okay?"

Lucy gave Savvy a sad smile before heading out the door, and Savvy waved back weakly before thumping down the hall.

This morning, Savvy had decided to ditch her crutches altogether. Now that her ankle wasn't quite so sensitive she could get around pretty well without them. Not good enough to hit the slopes, of course. But good enough. She wondered why they called it a "walking cast." What she was doing — *step, thunk, step, thunk* — didn't exactly resemble walking. A "lurching cast" would have been more like it.

Swinging the door wide open to the bright room, Savvy was nearly bowled over. She was not sure who was happier to see her, the Ski Wees or Carmen, who was standing in the middle of a clamoring circle trying to sort out who took who's hat.

"Savannah! You came back!" the older girl exclaimed. She almost sounded surprised.

"I said I would, didn't I?" Savvy smiled while several small sets of arms wrapped themselves around her legs. "Now, who wants to do some puzzles?" she asked. Three or four kids ran for the puzzle shelf. The two fighting about hats settled down with a game, and when the kids were all absorbed, Carmen took a moment to come over to talk to Savannah.

"You sure are good at calming kids down," she said appreciatively. "Do you think you're as good at cheering them up?" She raised her eyebrows and tilted her head toward the quiet corner and a large pile of cushions. Savvy looked at it, confused. Then she spotted a tiny Sorel boot sticking out. And a hand.

"Guess we're about to find out," Savannah said, working her cast over to the corner. Sliding down the wall, she sat beside the pillow pile. Slowly, she picked up one cushion at a time, tossing them aside until she could see a foot, a hand, two legs, a body, a pair of crossed arms, and a scowling face beneath a red-striped hat. Taking a closer look, Savvy spotted the reason for the frown. He had a cast on his left arm.

"Hey," Savvy said. "I'm Savvy."

The cast kid didn't respond.

"Um, hello?" Savvy tried again.

He wasn't talking.

Savvy's heart went out. She knew just how he felt — they were both saddled with casts. The rigid protection might be helping to knit their bones back together correctly, but they were also big, ugly reminders of all the fun they *weren't* having.

"See mine?" she asked, lifting her foot and

71

lowering it gently. "We match." The kid didn't smile, but his mouth twitched.

Suddenly, Savvy had an idea. She looked over at the craft cabinet in the far corner. The doors were labeled SCISSORS. GLUE. SCRAPS. TAPE. RULERS. STICKERS. MAGAZINES. She smiled at the silent kid who was still staring at her cast. "I want to show you something," she said conspiratorially. "But first you have to tell me your name."

The little boy hesitated for a minute, then leaned in close to Savannah. "Connor," he whispered.

"Nice to meet you, Connor," Savannah replied. "Are you ready to transform your cast?" She took his hand and led him over to the table by the craft cabinet, then pulled out a giant stack of ski and sport magazines.

"If you cut out your favorite pictures we can glue them onto your cast to make a collage. It'll be like wearing a cool piece of art on your arm — art that you made yourself!"

Connor's eyes lit up and he silently began to sift through the magazines. He liked car pictures best, and cut out all colors, sizes, and shapes of them. Savvy went for the winter sports action shots. They cut out pictures all morning, then got to work gluing — with lots of help — after lunch.

By the end of the day, Connor's cast was covered in clips, and it looked amazing. In fact, he was the envy of every Ski Wee in the room. When his parents came to pick him up he couldn't wait to show them, and they were thrilled with his good spirits.

"See you, Connor," Savvy said, hobbling over to say good-bye. "Nice cast," she added, smiling.

Connor smiled shyly. "Nice cast," he said, returning the compliment. Besides telling her his name, it was the only thing he'd said all day. And he was right. Her freshly collaged cast looked pretty ripping, too.

The room was almost all tidied up when Carmen told Savvy to go ahead and take off. "I can take care of the rest," she said, "as long as you promise to come back tomorrow."

"You know it," Savvy said. She was tired from the long day, but felt as good as she had since the accident. Cheering up Connor had cheered her up, too. But something was still bothering her. Pushing up her long sleeve to check the time, she realized what it was.

It was after four, and Lucy and Ellison hadn't come by.

Pushing open the door, Savvy looked down the long hallway. She hoped her friends were just late, that she would see them hurrying to catch her. They'd already missed the kids but if they got there soon they could at least see the place and meet Carmen. But the only people in the hall were skiers rushing out to get in a last run and families trying to gather everything together to go back to their cabins or condos.

Savvy let the door close and lingered inside, scraping glue off the table with her fingernail. When the door opened a minute later, she looked up excitedly, but it wasn't her friends. It was her aunt Tilly.

"Don't look so happy to see me," her aunt teased, giving Savannah a hug.

Savannah sighed. "Of course I'm happy to see you. I was just waiting for Lucy and Ellison, that's all."

"Ah, well, those are tough boots to fill," her aunt admitted. "But I did want to find out how that ankle is doing. I see you're off your crutches already." Savvy's aunt raised an eyebrow, asking without asking if that was really a good idea.

Savannah nodded. Her ankle had started to throb a little but she did not want to admit it. "Yeah. It feels great," she fibbed as Carmen approached.

"Hi, Tilly," Carmen said. "How's it going out on the slopes?"

"Not too bad today, for ski-week," Tilly replied. "How's it going in here?"

"It's going just fine, thanks to Savannah," Carmen replied. "She's been a lifesaver. But I can't seem to get her to clear out when she's supposed to. . . ." Carmen jangled her keys. "Time to lock up."

"I know when it's time to leave," Tilly said, slipping into the hall. "I'll see you soon, Savannah. Try and stay off of that ankle. Okay?"

Savvy gave her aunt a little wave and told Carmen she'd see her in the morning before heading to the shuttle stop. With the sun behind the mountains, the air was beyond chilly. Savvy shivered in her sweater and wished she had her jacket. When she'd let Ellison borrow it that morning she thought she'd have it back before it was time to go home. She shivered again as she showed her pass and climbed aboard the shuttle, wondering what had kept her friends away. Maybe Lucy was afraid of the tot snot. Maybe they just forgot.

Or maybe, just maybe, her friends were having more fun without her.

Chapter 8

Unglued

It was well after dark when Lucy and Ellison came stomping and stumbling into the cabin kitchen. Their eyes sparkled and their cheeks were red with cold.

"I have sore muscles on my sore muscles!" Ellison exclaimed, peeling off her jacket — Savannah's jacket — and plopping down on the couch next to her.

"I have bruises on my bruises," Lucy chimed in as she shook the snow from her hat. Despite their gripes, it was clear neither of them minded a single bit. They looked like they'd been having the time of their lives. "I feel like a noodle!" Lucy let her arms hang limp like cooked spaghetti to demonstrate.

"Too bad we're not having pasta," Savvy said, forcing a smile. She had been home for more than an hour, waiting and stewing.

"What are we having?" Ellison asked. She scanned the kitchen and answered her own question, spotting square boxes on the counter. "Mmm. Pizza. I could eat pizza all day."

That's good, because it looks like you'll have to, Savvy thought. She had asked for pizza tonight, and her mom had agreed. Pizza was the only thing they served at the Outpost, so Lucy and Ellison had already eaten some today, she knew. Secretly, Savvy was hoping they would be sick of it, and when both of her friends smiled at the idea of another slice, Savvy wished she had ordered anchovies.

"Hurry and change," Mrs. Heglund prompted the girls, coming into the kitchen. "Dinner's getting cold." She shooed them out of the room and followed them upstairs.

Mr. Heglund took a seat at the table. "How were the snow babies today?" he asked.

"Ski Wees," Savannah corrected. "They're not babies — they're little kids. And they were fine." She focused on setting the table, ignoring the laughter coming from upstairs. Fork. Knife. Napkin. Fork. Knife. Napkin.

When everyone had gathered around the table and helped themselves to a slice of Savvy's favorite — artichoke heart, mushroom, and sausage — they dug in.

"Yum." Ellison nodded. "This is the perfect combo, and I don't even like artichokes."

"Mmmm," Lucy agreed. "Way better than the Outpost."

Savvy forced a smile. Outpost pizza came out of a freezer and went right into the microwave. It was hardly gourmet. But Savvy was sure it would taste better than this. Her mood was tainting everything, and at the moment her favorite pizza tasted like an old sponge.

"I wish you could have been with us today," Lucy said. She looked anxiously at Savvy, and Savannah looked away.

"Yeah, you should have seen the wipeouts!" Ellison laughed. "Some of them went way beyond yard sales — they looked more like flea markets. Especially Lucy's!" Ellison gave Lucy a shove, and Lucy cringed and turned away.

"Bruise!" she yelped.

"Of course, nobody wiped out as well as you did, Savannah," Ellison blurted. As soon as the words were out of her mouth she looked guilty, like she wanted to grab them out of the air and shove them back in. "I mean, you managed to hang on to your stuff, but, uh, you have to admit. You kind of . . . took the cake," she backpedaled.

Savvy shrugged. "I bit it, all right."

"You're not the only one," Lucy said, hoping to soften the blow.

"Of course not," Mr. Heglund chimed in. "How do you think my sister pays the bills? She counts on crashes."

"One of the Ski Wees has a broken arm," Savvy offered, hoping to deflect a little attention. She felt bad enough without remembering that this whole sorry situation was her own fault. If she hadn't attempted such a stupid stunt in the first place, her ankle would be just fine and she wouldn't be hosting the world's biggest pity party in her head. And holding a grudge against her friends felt worse than her broken ankle. Lucy and Ellison hadn't done anything wrong — they'd just been having a good time. Wasn't that the reason Savannah had brought them up here to begin with?

"We decided to decorate them today. You know, to cheer ourselves up." Savvy smiled and lifted her cast up to show everyone.

"Wow!"

"Cool!"

The reaction was what she needed. Savvy could feel her spirits lift as she admired her own handiwork. She had to admit the paper-patchwork cast had turned out great.

"That looks amazing." Ellison reached over to touch the smooth collage.

"I think there's enough glue on here to make it waterproof," Savvy said with a laugh. She set her foot gingerly back down and took a big bite. Sprinkled with laughter, the pizza was delicious.

Savvy waited on the couch after dinner, carefully setting up the Scrabble board. She was getting around okay with her cast, but trucking up and down the stairs wasn't worth the effort until it was time to go to bed.

Overhead she could hear shuffling in the dorm — Ellison and Lucy putting on cozy clothes — and fidgeted, ready to start the game. The bag of square letter chips rattled as she tossed it back and forth between her hands. Taking a deep breath, she congratulated herself on letting go of being stood up. It just wasn't worth it to be mad. After all, she'd been the no-show at lunch with Ellison and Lucy the day before. And now, at least, they were all back together for the evening. The important thing, Savannah reminded herself, was to make the most of the time they had.

The dorm room door slammed and a second later, Lucy and Ellison thundered down the stairs.

Savannah's mouth dropped open. She was sprawled on the couch cushions in soft, slouchy pants and a huge sweatshirt. But her friends were dressed, glossed, and ready to go. There wasn't a pajama bottom in sight.

"Oh, I guess we forgot to tell you we're going skating tonight," Lucy said softly, registering the look on Savannah's face.

"Yeah. You should come! There are a bunch of kids going. . . ." Ellison was smiling, but her eyes looked a little pinched.

Savvy was silent. She looked at her friends, then at her leg, and back at her friends.

"I mean to watch," Ellison said with a gulp. "We could bring you hot chocolate, and take turns hanging out with you in the lodge. . . ."

Savvy stared at her cast. She'd already spent way too much time hanging out in the lodge this trip. Besides, she was not the spectator type. She was a participant — accustomed to being in the middle of it all. "You go ahead," she said tightly. "Mom and I were planning to play a little Scrabble."

"That sounds fun," Lucy said, a little too brightly and with a wide smile. Savvy did not return her grin.

The door closed behind Savvy's best friends and her resolve to put her bad feelings behind her disappeared. Anger bubbled up in her chest. It wasn't enough that Lucy and Ellison had spent the whole day without her on the slopes. Now they were going skating without her, too! They'd chosen *another* activity that left her out in the cold. And they hadn't even bothered to tell her about it until they were practically out the door.

Feeling miserable, Savannah noticed that a couple of her cast collage pictures were starting to curl up, coming unglued. That was exactly how she felt — unglued. Unglued and alone. She angrily tore off a curling scrap and let it flutter to the floor.

Savannah slammed the game board shut and shoved it back into the box before standing up. The partially open bag of letters slid off her lap, and the wooden pieces scattered all over the floor next to the collage scrap. Well, too bad! There was no way she was crawling around to gather the mess up. Leaving the pieces where they were, Savvy thumped up the stairs.

In the dorm room she changed into her pajamas and brushed her teeth, angrily thrusting the brush back and forth. *How could they? How could they??*

Snuggled under her covers, Savvy tossed and turned. It was too early for sleep. Too late for fun. Her eyes filled with hot tears and she felt more alone than she could remember. It was almost her birthday! She was in Tahoe with her friends! At least, they were supposed to be her friends.

Warm, wet tears slid down Savvy's cheeks as she stared up at the ski posters. Lucy and Ellison left her so easily, abandoned her after she invited them up here for the week and everything.

Savannah lay there for what seemed like forever, wallowing in her misery. She must have fallen asleep at some point because the next thing she knew the door was opening. A shaft of light widened across the ceiling. She heard whispering voices.

"Savvy? You awake?"

Not to you, I'm not, Savannah thought. She rolled over so they couldn't see her face and kept her mouth and eyes shut.

No, she wasn't the slightest bit awake.

Chapter 9

Out in the cold

As soon as Savvy opened her eyes the next morning, an avalanche of bad feelings pressed down on her chest. Everything felt wrong! Quietly climbing out of bed, she pulled some stretchy fleece pants and a long-sleeved shirt out of her duffel. Her friends were just waking up when Savannah poked her head through a patterned fleece V-neck, and though they both offered a bleary good morning, Savannah did not reply. Why should she talk to them after they abandoned her? Well, she might talk to them someday — right after they apologized for their terrible behavior and begged her for forgiveness.

Hurrying down to the kitchen, Savvy poured herself a bowl of cereal and dumped in some milk.

She was slurping up the last bit when her friends appeared, looking cheerful in their bibs and sweaters.

"Everything all right?" Lucy asked lightly.

Savannah pondered this for half a second. *Um, no*, she thought. *Everything is not all right.* In fact, everything was pretty terrible. How could her two best friends not see that? She picked miserably at one of the loosening collage pieces (there were several now). The words under the idyllic winter picture read WINTER WONDERLAND. Savvy tried to ignore the lump in her stomach.

"Sure, everything's dandy," Savannah said sarcastically. She just wanted her friends to tell her they were sorry, that they missed her the night before on the rink, or even how grateful they were to Savannah for bringing them up here for the week. But they didn't. So Savvy carried her bowl to the sink, grabbed her hat, mittens, and her ski jacket (Ellison definitely wouldn't be wearing *that* today), and headed outside to catch the early shuttle bus. Her friends might not want her around, but she knew a bunch of little kids who did, and Carmen, too.

Fifteen minutes later, Savannah hobbled off the bus and scanned the early-bird crowd for Eric, hoping to spot his bright orange ski cap near the bottom of the mountain. She wanted to see his friendly face, to hear him call her "Shredder," to hang out with him for a few minutes. He hadn't seen her cast, and she hadn't had a chance to invite him to her birthday dinner. She needed to make sure he would be there, especially since it didn't look like she'd be celebrating with her girlfriends!

Savvy was still scanning the vicinity for Eric when a small bundle ran up to her waving a familiar and very artistic-looking arm. Connor looked happier than Savvy had ever seen him, and he even gave her knee a little squeeze.

"We can't thank you enough," his dad said, catching up and extending a hand in Savannah's direction. "Thanks to you our little guy is back to his old self again, broken arm and all."

Savvy smiled down at Connor, who was gently flicking the peeling pictures on her cast. "No problem," she said. "It's always good to have a cast buddy — especially when you need to turn it into a work of wearable art. Right, Connor?"

Connor nodded emphatically and reached his hand up to grab Savvy's finger.

"We were wondering if you might be available to babysit tonight," Connor's dad went on. "We have a dinner planned, and Connor said grown-ups are boring and he would rather spend the evening with you."

"Is that so?" Savannah asked, gazing down at her new friend. "You said all that?"

Connor nodded again.

"It would be from six to ten," Connor's dad offered up the details. "How does sixty dollars sound?"

Sixty dollars in one night! Savannah thought. That was exactly what she needed to get that gorgeous green snowboard. And with a little luck, her ankle would heal on schedule and she'd be able to hit the slopes before the snow melted this season!

"That sounds great," Savannah said excitedly. This was by far the best thing that had happened to her in days. It even gave her a little glimmer of hope that her slump was coming to an end.

Connor's dad jotted down the address of the house they were staying in and handed it to Savannah. Then he gave Connor a hug goodbye. "See you later, buddy," he said, tousling his son's hair.

As soon as Connor's dad was out the door, Savannah announced that she and Connor had some work to do. "I need you to help me fix my cast." She wasn't feeling unglued any longer. Her cast shouldn't be either. Connor eyed her peeling collage with concern and nodded seriously. A few minutes later they had recruited a couple of kids to help. Within half an hour Savannah's cast was covered with another layer and every single snowy image was firmly attached. Winter Wonderland was back in action.

Savannah kept her eyes peeled for Eric all day, to no avail. She was beginning to think she'd have to go stand at the bottom of the ski hill when he walked right by the Ski Wee room.

"Eric!" she called, waving excitedly.

For a second he looked like he didn't recognize her, then he ambled over, raising his chin slightly in greeting.

"Hey." He smiled and brushed back his shaggy hair. He wasn't wearing a hat, and one of his curls was pointing to a dimple in his right cheek.

"Are you a sight for sore eyes!" Savannah said. She wondered why she'd never noticed the dimple before and forced herself to look away. "I've been looking for you all day," she said to the floor.

"Oh, uh, sorry," Eric replied. He shoved his hands deep in his pockets and began to rock back and forth on his heels.

"I was wondering if you have any big plans tomorrow."

Eric looked over his shoulder like he was expecting to see someone. "Tomorrow?" he echoed. "Um, well . . ." Turning back, he avoided Savvy's gaze and looked down at his feet. "Can I get back to you?"

Savannah was suddenly overwhelmed by a really uncomfortable feeling. Eric wasn't acting like his easygoing self. Or even like they were friends. He was acting like he couldn't wait to get away from her.

"Oops, I have to go," he mumbled. He looked at his watch — *after* he said he had to leave — then without looking her in the eye, he turned, waved, and made a beeline down the hall so fast his unzipped ski-instructor jacket flapped at his sides.

Savannah felt the room tilt as she watched him rush away. What happened to the friend she'd skied with since she was five? Why were her girlfriends turning against her? Tomorrow was her birthday, and she felt totally, completely alone.

Babysitting that night cheered Savannah more than she wished it had to. Never did she think she would have been so happy to eat dinosaur-shaped chicken nuggets and watch *Care Bears* (twice) on a portable DVD player. But it beat lying around at the cabin watching her friends prepare for yet another night of fun without her. She didn't bother to tell them where she was going either. After calling her mom to let her know that she had a babysitting job, she made up an excuse to stay at the lodge until it was time to take the shuttle to Connor's.

Connor lit up when she walked in, and chatted all through dinner. Apparently, once the kid found his tongue he didn't stop using it. Savvy didn't mind the chatter — it kept her mind off other things. She let him ramble, put on the movie, and halfway through the second *Care Bear* screening he fell asleep on the couch with his head on her arm. Savvy made sure the Bears got back to Care-a-Lot for the second time. Then she lugged him to his bed and tucked him in.

"Good night," she whispered, pulling the comforter up to the kid's chin.

"Sleep tight," Connor whispered back.

Later, when Connor's dad dropped Savannah off at her cabin, Lucy and Ellison were in the living room watching *Mean Girls* on TV.

How appropriate, Savannah thought as she snuck in behind them, half hoping they would notice her and half hoping they wouldn't. As luck would have it, they were too absorbed in the movie to see her, so she made her way up the stairs feeling slightly invisible, and slightly miserable, too.

When the girls came into the dorm later, Savvy was still awake — she'd been wrestling with her bedclothes and her emotions for more than an hour. Though she'd been trying to hold on to the cozy evening with Connor and the excitement of having all the cash she needed for her board, she could not keep the bad feelings at bay. There was a damp spot on her pillow, her nose was stuffy, and her head ached from crying. Not that she wanted her so-called friends to know any of that.

"Hey, when did Savvy get back? I didn't even hear her come in," Lucy whispered.

"I don't think she's talking to us," Ellison said. Her hushed voice sounded worried. Her shoes thunked to the ground.

"I don't either. She's been acting weird all day," Lucy replied in a nightgown-muffled voice.

Ellison's voice drifted up from the low trundle bed. "Maybe it's better this way. At least now we know she won't find out."

Find out what? Savannah's mind reeled.

"I think it's safe so long as Eric doesn't say

91

anything," Ellison continued, whispering into the darkness. "Some guys are really bad at keeping secrets, though."

Savannah's heart hammered as she listened to the sounds of the girls settling into their beds. She waited for them to say more, but they didn't. She swallowed quietly and when the room fell silent she let a warm tear drift down to her pillow to land on the already salt-soaked spot. It was obvious. Just when she realized that she had a crush on her old friend, he seemed to have developed a thing for Ellison. Clearly they were hanging out. They probably had plans tomorrow, on *her* birthday, and that must have been why Eric had acted so weird that afternoon. Worse, Ellison didn't want her to know, and Lucy was in on it.

Savannah made a mental addition to the list of hurts that were rapidly accumulating: "Betrayed" now made the list, right after "hurt" and "abandoned."

And it wasn't just Ellison and Lucy either. It was Eric. She couldn't get the image of him racing down the hall away from her out of her head.

Savvy furtively glanced at the illuminated numbers on the bedside clock, which read 11:02. In less than an hour, it would be her birthday.

The worst birthday of her life.

Chapter 10

Birthday Blues

The next morning, Savannah was awakened by an intense itch underneath her cast — an itch she couldn't scratch. Pulling open her bedside table drawer, she grabbed a ballpoint pen, shoved it between her calf and her cast, and scratched like crazy. Arrgh! It didn't reach!

"Darn it!" Savannah growled. She looked around the room for something longer and realized:

1) She was alone,
2) it was her birthday, and
3) there was nothing long and skinny enough for her to scratch the itch that was making her insane.

Savannah resisted the urge to lie back down and pull her pillow over her head, and threw the covers aside instead. Once her feet were on the floor the itch subsided a little and she decided her friends and her parents were probably waiting downstairs with her favorite breakfast — blueberry pancakes with powdered sugar and whipped cream. She was pretty sure she could smell the blueberries. . . .

After pulling on the best possible birthday outfit she could wear with her cast — clean sweats and a cashmere sweater — and quickly brushing her hair, Savannah made her way to the kitchen. She was still bristling at her friends, but now that it was her actual birthday she was hoping that being treated like a queen would make her feel better. There was no way they could leave her out today, right?

Wrong! Standing in the doorway, Savannah stared into the empty kitchen. The table was set with a single setting, and a note sat atop the plate.

Happy Birthday, Sweetie!
We decided to let you sleep in, but couldn't wait any longer. I had to run into town to pick up a few things. The girls left early for the mountain. They didn't want to wake you either. Your favorite pancakes are in the oven. See you at the lodge later.

Love, Mom

Savannah stared at the note in disbelief. "Are they kidding?" she asked the empty room, knowing, of course, that they were not. She could feel her fury bubbling inside her along with more hot tears. Neither her parents nor her best friends could wait around for her *on her birthday*? And where were the cards and presents? She pulled a dried-out pancake from the oven, nibbled the crusty edge, and tossed it into the sink. "It's only ten o'clock," she announced to the digital clock over the stove. Then, as the time sunk in, alarm overtook her anger. Ten o'clock! Oh no, she was late!

Grabbing her jacket and hat, she lurched out the door to the shuttle stop, barely noticing that it was yet another gorgeous day with a clear blue sky. Savvy greeted the shuttle driver and took a seat right near the front so she would be one of the first passengers off when they arrived at the lodge. Time seemed to pass super-slowly as the shuttle stopped at practically every corner to pick up the skiers and snowboarders who were headed for the mountain.

By the time Savvy got to the Ski Wee room in the lodge, it was after ten thirty. "I'm so sorry," she said breathlessly as several of the kids bowled her over with hugs. "I totally overslept."

"That's okay, I'm just glad you're here!" Carmen

said, untangling herself from a pair of rambunctious preschoolers. "I figured you would show up today, though." Carmen held out an envelope.

Savvy grabbed it and tore it open, wondering why Carmen thought working on your birthday was a good thing. But when the contents of the envelope slid into her hand, Savvy realized Carmen wasn't giving her a card, she'd just handed her a check. Her first paycheck!

Before she could get too excited about having enough scratch to buy her board and a new pair of sunglasses, Connor tugged at Savannah's hand and brought her back to reality. He led her over to the craft table, where a group of kids had been hard at work cutting out more magazine pictures. Their cast decorating had started a collage craze! Savannah tucked her check safely away (nobody would be cutting that up anytime soon) and set out giant pieces of thick paper, glue, and paintbrushes and let the kids go at it.

Before long, it was lunchtime, and after the kids had filled their bellies with fruit, sandwiches, and chips, it was time for some of them to head outside for lessons.

"I need you to take Gretchen, Nicholas, Sam, Natalie, and Abigail. You know where the meeting place is, right?" Carmen asked as she dropped a giant pile of cold-weather gear on the table in the middle of the room.

Savannah smiled, remembering the dozens of times she'd met up with her first instructors under the red sign with the brass bell for her own lessons when she was little. "Of course," she replied as she sifted through the pile of fleece and down, starting the chaotic process of getting the kids ready for the slopes.

Fifteen minutes later, she was buckling the last ski boot and getting the last helmet fitted onto a little head. "Come on, troops," she called. "Let's get outside before you all overheat."

They trudged through the dining area of the lodge and out into the wintry sunshine. No sooner had they gotten to their designated meeting place than Gretchen tugged on Savvy's hand.

"I have to go potty," she whispered, trying to cross her legs in her pink snow pants and scrunching up her round face. "Really bad."

Savannah quickly tracked down the group instructor and told her she'd be back with her fifth student in a few minutes. "Come on," she said to Gretchen, taking her by the hand. Moving as quickly as she could in her walking cast, Savannah led the way to the nearest bathroom, which suddenly seemed very far away.

"I can't hold it!" Gretchen squeaked as Savvy gently pushed her into a stall and pulled the door closed. After several long seconds of silence Gretchen's little voice came through the door. "I need help."

Half in shock and half feeling like an idiot for assuming a four-year-old could get out of her own snow gear when she really had to pee, Savannah pulled open the door. The last thing she wanted to deal with was a puddle on the bathroom floor! Crouching down, she pulled off Gretchen's mittens, unzipped her jacket, and unsnapped her bibs.

"Thanks," Gretchen sighed as she pulled down her pants and long johns and lifted herself onto the seat.

As she watched the little girl reach for the toilet paper Savannah marveled at the fact that she was squeezed into a bathroom stall with a four-year-old on the afternoon of her twelfth birthday. And then, even more surprising, she realized that she was smiling. Helping somebody go to the toilet was, so far, the highlight of her birthday. "You're welcome," she said, and meant it.

Once Gretchen was all geared up again, Savvy escorted her outside for her lesson. In the bright sun, the temperature was warm enough to take the edge off but not so warm that it turned the snow to mashed potatoes. Snow-frosted trees dotted the mountain along with the brightly colored jackets of skiers and snowboarders. Savannah breathed in the crisp air and smiled at the world.

"Look!" Gretchen cried, pointing. "It's one of Frosty's friends!"

Savannah chuckled to herself as she spied the giant snow groomer Gretchen was referring to. "Well, whaddya know," she marveled with a grin.

Just then she spied something else — Ellison and Lucy coming down the mountain. They looked great as they weaved through the other boarders, carving neat turns. Lucy had come so far since the first day it was amazing, and Ellison looked like she was born to board! Savannah wanted desperately to talk to them, to tell them how fabulous they looked on the slopes, that she wasn't mad anymore, that her birthday was going pretty well, and that she finally had enough money to buy her beautiful snowboard! And she was sure that they had giant birthday hugs — and apologies — for her, too.

Savannah was just raising her hand to wave to her friends when they both slid to a stop next to Eric, who she hadn't noticed standing near the chairlift.

"Biff!" Eric grinned and slapped Ellison on the back.

Savvy winced. Eric had given Ellison a nickname. And as she watched the three huddle up like good friends sharing a great secret, her heart sank to her knees. They were probably telling each other how lucky they were that she, Shredder, was not around to bore them with her tips and tricks. And did Eric have to leave his hand on Ellison's shoulder?

The bad feelings came screaming back with a vengeance and Savannah felt all the hurt and anger wash over her for what felt like the hundredth time. Turning quickly and nudging Gretchen toward the other kids in her lesson, she kept her back to her former friends, doing her best to pretend she hadn't seen them at all.

Chapter 11

Wipeout

The ski instructor leaned over his poles and eyed his five small charges. His face split into a wide grin. "Who's ready to ride a magic carpet?" he asked. Four of the kids squealed and started scooching their little skis along the snow toward the black "carpet" that would transport them to the top of the mild slope. Gretchen squeezed Savvy's hand tighter, and Savvy was glad. After seeing Lucy and Ellison putting their heads together with Eric, she needed someone to hold her hand as much as the nervous four-year-old did.

"What if I fall?" Gretchen whimpered.

"Snow's not too hard," Savvy assured her, hoping Gretchen would not point out the fact that she had broken her ankle falling on the not-too-hard snow.

"I mean, what if I fall down, down, down off the carpet when it's flying?" Gretchen said in a tiny voice.

Savannah nearly laughed out loud, but stopped herself when she saw the solemn look on Gretchen's little face. Her fears were no joke, and neither was the kid's imagination! "The 'flying carpet' is just a name. It's really just a big piece of rubber that moves around a giant track set on the ground. It won't take off, I promise."

The mittened vice on Savvy's hand relaxed, and Savannah urged Gretchen to follow the others to the moving mat. She stayed, waving until the kids were heading upward, then slowly turned around. Her friends were nowhere in sight, and Savvy realized she wasn't sure which was harder to take, seeing her friends huddled together, Eric's hand on Ellison's arm . . . or not seeing them at all. Savvy suspected they'd spotted her and headed someplace else to whisper about how dumb she was for showing off, or maybe how all her new friends were under five feet tall and five years old. It was hard, even for Savvy, to believe that she used to rule these slopes. She felt like a pile of dirty slush kicked off somebody's boot in the parking lot.

Pity isn't pretty, she told herself, wishing she could just get over the whole thing. She pushed her hands into her pockets and felt the wad of cash she had taken from her drawer that morning. Suddenly, she knew what would make her feel better. Carmen would be waiting for her back in the lodge, but a quick detour to the ski shop wouldn't hurt. And a present — even one she bought for herself — might bring on the birthday feeling that was sadly lacking from Savvy's day.

By taking a little hop each time she stepped on her good ankle, Savvy could get some decent walking speed, especially once she was off the snow. She hustled off the hill, down the wooden boardwalk, and into the ski shop, which was bustling with lunchtime shoppers. She scanned the store quickly for Hector and saw him taking ginormous sunglasses out of the glass case for a woman dressed in all white with big white Wookiee boots on her feet. She looked pretty high maintenance — Hector could be a while.

"Can I help you?" one of the other ski-shop workers asked, smiling at Savvy.

"Um, yeah. I'd like —" Savvy stopped. The hand

she was about to point with dropped to her side. Her mouth went dry. The wall behind the main counter, where her board usually hung, was empty. The light green Burton of her dreams wasn't there. Savannah looked around frantically, checking all the other walls. Her board was nowhere to be seen.

"Yes?" The clerk, one of the few people at the shop that Savvy had never seen before, looked at her expectantly.

"Have you seen the board that used to be right there?" Savvy asked, still scanning and trying to remain calm. Maybe someone had taken it down to look at it.

"Yeah, wasn't it green or something?" The guy scratched his bristly chin.

"Yes. Light green. It was a Burton. This year's model. And you only had one of them. Did you move it?"

"Hmm. I don't think so," he answered slowly. "Hec, you know what happened to that Burton?" Bristle-chin shouted across the shop.

Hector looked up from the sunglass case where he was crouching. Well over a dozen pairs of glasses were lying on top of the glass and the white-on-white woman was pointing at yet another pair.

"Sold it," Hector shouted back. "Just a tick ago." When he stood up, he spotted Savannah and his expression changed. His eyes went soft and he smiled feebly. "Sorry, luv. Some bloke got it," he said softly. "Lots of other lovely boards here, though."

Savvy was speechless. She curled her fingers tightly around the wad of money in her pocket and tried unsuccessfully to gulp down the lump in her throat. "No worries," she said, her voice breaking.

"We might be able to place a special order," the clerk offered. "We could get it here in, oh, five weeks?"

Five weeks was a lifetime. It would practically be April by then! Savvy shook her head and bit down on her bottom lip. Her dream of bettering her birthday and getting the board before the end of the season melted away, and she limped out of the store without even waving good-bye.

If she weren't already down to one good leg, Savvy would have kicked the wall. It was so unfair! This was supposed to be an amazing birthday! Not to mention that it was probably her only chance to have her friends along for ski-week. And now? She already had to forget skiing, boarding, and skating. Forget the queen-of-the-hill feeling of being up on the mountain. Forget hanging out with her friends in the Alpine sun. Her friends had already forgotten *her*, that was obvious. And adding insult to injury, her dream board belonged to someone else. Even her silver lining was tarnished.

Savvy wished she could hurl herself facedown in a snowbank and sulk until her birthday was over or her face froze off, whichever came first. Unfortunately, Carmen was still waiting for her along with a dozen sticky Ski Wees. Left with no choice, she limped dejectedly back into the lodge.

Chapter 12

Friday Night Lights

By the time the last parent picked up the last Ski Wee, Savannah was seriously dragging bottom. As she limped toward the shuttle stop, tired and alone, she felt certain that nobody in Heglund family history had ever had a worse birthday than she was having right now. *At least you've got that*, she thought to herself. *At least you're the best at being the worst.*

During lunch, one of the Ski Wees had spilled a Capri Sun all over her cast, dissolving the glue, and now, as she made her way across the snow, tropical-punch-stained pieces of Savvy's winter dream slipped off into the dirty white drifts.

The best thing to do now, Savvy figured, the *only* thing to do now . . . was to forget that it was her birthday at all. Everyone else had! Next year when her ankle was all healed she could try again. The thought didn't offer a lot of comfort.

The shuttle stop was empty and Savvy sat down to wait on the chilly bench. Cold seeped up through her seat. She felt more tired than she did after a full day of half-pipe. She wasn't sure what was exhausting her so much — the kids or the disappointment. Either way, she was looking forward to a hot shower (with her leg carefully enclosed in a Hefty garbage bag) and a warm bed.

The shuttle had just hissed to a stop when she heard voices behind her.

"Savvy!" That was Ellison.

"Savannah!" And then Lucy.

"Wait!"

"Don't get on that bus!" This last request sounded a little desperate.

Savannah was tempted to climb aboard and pretend she hadn't heard anything, but her friends had already pretty much caught up with her, and it was not as if she could make a speedy getaway. So Savvy waved the driver on, and turned to face Lucy and Ellison, who were red-faced and out of breath.

"Wow. Running in ski boots is *hard*," Ellison

wheezed as she bent over to rub her leg. "I think I sprained my shin."

"You can't sprain your shin," Lucy said, whacking Ellison lightly. "Come on. Tell her."

Lucy and Ellison were both smiling widely as they crunched closer. "You tell her," Ellison said.

Savvy could see something was up. Ellison liked to tell everything — and if she was as flipped for Eric as it appeared, well, it didn't make any sense that she wouldn't want to blab it to the mountaintops. But Savvy never would have guessed that her friends would actually enjoy bursting her bubble this much. She was beginning to wish she'd gotten on the shuttle.

"What?" Savannah asked with her hands on her hips. "Did you track me down to tell me about your big plans with Eric tonight, *Biff*?"

"I told you she knew!" Ellison whacked Lucy back.

But Lucy ignored it. Her big eyes grew wider and she flipped her hair. "Savvy, we've been looking all over for you," she said, coming closer. She linked her arm through Savannah's and started to lead her from the shuttle shelter. "We need you."

Ellison linked up with Savvy on the other side. She was trapped. The girls wanted something, and it was pretty obvious they had completely forgotten about her birthday.

"It'll only take a minute," Ellison added as they rounded the back of lodge. At the base of the chairlift, where the three of them had ridden the first day, was a small hut set up for Ski Patrol. It was where the patrollers kept their gear and the main radio so they could report about what was happening anywhere on the mountain. Savvy had been inside it with her aunt several times, and for a second she thought maybe her aunt had remembered it was her birthday and had asked her friends to get her.

But when the door to the hut opened, Tilly wasn't there. Eric stepped out and leaned against the jamb. His laid-back, lopsided smile was back. "Hey, Shredder, how about a run?" he asked casually, looking right at Savannah. Savvy looked back at Eric like he'd experienced one too many brain freezes, pointed at her bulky cast, and raised her eyebrows. Without a word, Eric gestured toward the snowmobile parked beside the hut. Lashed behind the small vehicle was a familiar-looking toboggan — the same kind Savvy had ridden off the slopes when she hurt herself. "The mountain has been missing you." He shrugged. "So have I." He dangled a set of keys. "Ready?"

Savvy hesitated. "Sure you don't want to take *Biff*?" she asked pointedly — her feelings were still sore.

Eric laughed. "She's good at falling. I'll give you that. But you have it all over her when it comes to tearing it up. No offense." Eric shot a look Ellison's way.

"None taken." Ellison grinned. "We all know Shredder's a snowbeast — when she's not in a cast. Now load up. Your chariot awaits."

Lucy gave Savannah a little shove and she took a step toward the, uh, chariot. "Go on," Lucy urged. "As my best friend once told me, you can't come down if you don't go up."

It seemed like a zillion years ago that Savvy was coaxing Lucy onto the slopes. Had it really only been a few days? Without another word, Savvy stepped into the toboggan and took a seat while Eric slid the key into the ignition. As soon as she was settled, he gunned the engine.

"See you at the top!" Lucy called. Eric wheeled the snowmobile in a slow circle and accelerated up the mountain while Lucy and Ellison strapped on their gear and quickly made their way to the chairlift.

Grateful for her multiple layers and her cozy fleece hat, Savvy watched her friends grow smaller

111

and smaller as the toboggan bounced higher and higher, making its way up the mountain. More than once she was glad to have the safety straps holding her in. She was a demon for speed, but she didn't usually take it lying down!

The light on the white hillsides was changing and as they came to the crest of the hill and Eric killed the engine, Savvy saw the sun beginning to set. The massive orange ball lit the slopes and turned the trees to shadowy silhouettes before it disappeared behind the white mountain ridge, leaving a glow behind. The view was absolutely breathtaking.

"Happy birthday, Savannah," he said quietly. He had climbed off the snowmobile and was crouched beside her on the snow. It was the first time in ages that he had used her real name.

Before the last sliver of orange was gone, Lucy and Ellison slid up beside them. Lucy pulled a thermos of hot chocolate out of her pack and poured a cup for everyone.

"A birthday toast!" she said, holding her cup high.

"Good-bye eleven and hello twelve!" Ellison said, sloshing a little bit of the chocolate onto the snow.

Eric helped Savannah struggle to her feet. Her

butt was turning to ice, but she didn't care. She held her cup together with the others and toasted her birthday.

"So, are you ready for your birthday ride down the mountain?" Lucy and Ellison asked in unison. Savannah gulped. The ride up had been a little nerve-racking. Riding down in the dark sounded, well, scary.

Just then the night-ski floodlights switched on and music poured out of giant speakers mounted on the trees. Savvy had almost forgotten about Friday Night Lights. It was when Powderbowl allowed night skiing on a couple of slopes and lit the place like it was a Christmas tree.

"I can take it from here." Aunt Tilly had appeared from out of nowhere and quickly unlashed the toboggan from the snowmobile. She held her hand out to Eric for the keys.

"You're not going to just set me loose, are you?" Savvy asked a little nervously. She could see herself hurtling down the mountain in the metal toboggan with no brakes, careening straight through the lodge and into the parking lot on the other side, where sparks would fly from beneath the scraping sled just like in the cartoons.

"Don't you worry," Eric assured her. "I'll be your sled dog for this run." He stepped into his skis, which Savvy hadn't even noticed until that moment.

The next thing Savannah knew, Ellison and Lucy were taking off their boards and handing them to her aunt to haul off the hill. They sat down on the toboggan, front and back, and made room for Savvy in the middle.

"Nobody should be alone on their birthday," Ellison explained while Savvy squeezed between them. The evening air was getting colder by the second but Savvy was warmer than she had been all day. Eric took the bars at the front of the toboggan and began to slowly steer them down the hill ski-patrol style.

The song pumping out of the speakers ended and a new one started — one of Savvy's favorites. Savannah sang along softly, soaking up the moment. First Ellison and then Lucy joined in until all of them were belting out the ballad. Even Eric sang along as he snake-turned slowly down the mountain, keeping his need for speed under wraps and letting the girls take it all in. It was a far cry from Savvy's last ride of the hill!

As the very first star twinkled into view, Savannah felt sparkly herself. Surrounded by friends, the song, the snow, the sky . . . the feeling went way beyond birthday. It felt like magic.

Chapter 13

Epic

When the birthday sled arrived at the bottom of the mountain, Savannah spotted her parents sitting at a big table by the window in the lodge dining room. Expertly steering the sled right up to the door, Eric came to a slow halt. "Your birthday banquet awaits, Shredder Queen," he said with his lopsided smile.

Lucy and Ellison helped Savvy get to her feet while Eric gallantly held the door open. On the other side of the glass, streamers and balloons hung over the giant table where her parents were sitting. Savannah's parents were smiling broadly.

"Happy birthday!" they called as the four friends entered the dining room. And no sooner had Savannah settled herself at the table than an entire pack of guests traipsed into the dining room — Carmen, Connor, Gretchen, Aunt Tilly, and Hector from the ski shop. Savvy seriously felt like royalty.

Connor was on her lap in a second. "Happy birthday," he whispered, pulling a homemade card out of his pocket. The whole cover was a collage showing all kinds of winter mountain scenes. On the inside he had written Happy Birthday Savvy in crooked letters and signed his name.

"I love it," Savannah declared, giving him a squeeze.

Connor beamed up at her. "I love *you*," he whispered back before sliding off her lap and finding a seat next to Carmen and Gretchen.

Wow, Savvy thought with a laugh. *This is the first time a cute boy's ever told me he loves me — and on my birthday, too!*

"What'll it be, birthday girl?" Savannah's dad asked as he skimmed the menu.

She knew exactly what she wanted. "I'll have the fondue!" she said. "To share. And lobster," she said, knowing her dad would not deny her the pricey treat tonight.

"And French fries!" Gretchen piped up, making everyone laugh.

The hubbub during dinner was a happy one and Savannah found herself looking around the table throughout the meal. Everyone was there — her family, her friends — new and old, big and small. And they were celebrating her. It was epic.

Everyone ate heartily — especially Savannah, who was sure it was the best lobster she had ever tasted. Then, in what seemed like a blur, the dishes had been cleared and the waitress was carrying in a giant light-green-and-white birthday cake illuminated by twelve tall candles. Savvy saw that it was in the shape of a snowboard, and smiled sadly in spite of herself. She couldn't help but remember that this snowboard made of flour and sugar was the only one she'd get this year.

Once Savannah blew out all the candles — in a single breath — pieces of chocolate cake were passed around with vanilla or coffee ice cream to top it off. Savannah bit off the end of the cake-snowboard and silently bid her dream board good-bye. Her birthday had been getting better and better. She did not want to get off track again.

"Are you okay, sweetie?" Savannah's dad asked, leaning across the table.

Savannah smiled, inwardly kicking herself for

wallowing when she had so many amazing people in her life and so much to be grateful for.

"I'm better than okay, Dad," she replied.

Then, out of the corner of her eye, Savvy saw Hector eat his last bite of cake, push his chair back, and walk out of the dining room. She hoped he wasn't leaving without saying good-bye.

"Good," Savannah's dad said. "I wouldn't want my girl to be sad on her birthday."

Savannah was barely listening because, as suddenly as he'd gone, Hector had reappeared carrying a very large, very interestingly shaped package wrapped in brown craft paper and tied with a giant bow. Savannah's heart skipped a beat as he carried the package toward her. It couldn't be. . . .

Hector leaned the package up against the window right next to Savannah. "Happy birthday, luv," he said, giving her a smooch on the cheek.

Savannah stared at the package. Then, in a sudden burst, she ripped off the paper. It was her beautiful green snowboard!

"I can't believe it!" she cried, hugging the board. "But you said —"

Hector's eyes twinkled. "I told you some bloke came in and bought it," Hector confirmed.

"What I didn't tell you was that the bloke was your dad!"

"Happy birthday, Savannah," her parents said in unison.

Savannah scrambled to her feet and threw her arms around her parents. "You guys are the best!" she cried. "Thank you so much!"

Chapter 14

Best Birthday Ever

Savvy forked up her last bite of cake and ice cream and sighed contentedly. Her friends, her family, the lobster, the cake . . . and her snowboard! She was so happy it was finally hers, she didn't even mind that she wouldn't be able to ride it for several weeks. She knew it would be a ride worth waiting for.

"Watch out!" Eric said, eyeing the board. "Once Shredder gets out there on her new Burton, there'll be no stopping her!"

"I'll give you a run for your money, that's for sure," Savannah vowed with a grin.

"I'm looking forward to it," he said.

"Is it everything you'd hoped for?" Ellison

asked before polishing off her soda and setting down her glass.

"And more!" Savannah said. "Especially because . . ." She leaned in close to her friends. It actually seemed really funny to her now. "I thought everyone forgot."

Ellison and Lucy burst out laughing. "Forgot . . . your birthday?" they said between gasps. "Savvy, we value our lives too much to do that!"

She laughed right along with them, seeing their point. She wasn't exactly the kind of girl who took birthdays lightly.

Suddenly, Lucy grew serious. "We're sorry we kept everything a secret," she said solemnly. "But we really wanted to surprise you."

"Well, you definitely did that," Savannah assured them. "I was so mad. . . ."

"And now?" Ellison asked.

"I'll never doubt you again."

"Good," Ellison said, getting to her feet. "Because there's just one more thing . . ."

"What?" Savvy was completely shocked. "There's more?"

"Indeed," Eric confirmed, rising from the table and heading toward the door. Ellison and Lucy linked arms with Savannah and escorted her out of the lodge to the skating rink. At first Savannah was confused. She couldn't skate! But then she spotted it — a birthday throne waiting for her on the edge of the rink. When she looked closely, she could see that it was really just a plastic cafeteria chair underneath, but it had been decorated with streamers, balloons, and tinsel, and had a velvet cushion on the seat.

"Your crown, my queen," Ellison said, holding out a lovely headpiece made of a delicate wire garland affixed to a ridiculous jester-style snow hat. Savannah slipped the crown onto her head and sat down in the chair.

"We can't spin as fast as you do," Lucy said as she quickly laced up her skates. "But that doesn't mean we can't take you for a royal ride."

With everyone's boots snugly tied, Eric started to skate. He pushed Savannah in wide circles across the ice while her friends flanked her on either side. She was amazed at how easily the metal-footed chair legs slid over the smooth ice. It felt like she was floating! As they completed the first lap around the ice, Connor and Gretchen came flying out the door, asking for a ride.

"You can take turns," Savvy told them as Gretchen climbed onto her lap. With Lucy at the helm they headed off on another loop, making wide zigzags all around the rink. Gretchen giggled all the way, hanging on tightly to Savannah's arms. Then it was Connor's turn, and Ellison pushed. By the time they got around the rink, Carmen was outside, ready to take the tired kids home.

"Bye, Savvy," they said, giving her birthday hugs and then waving their mittened hands through the air. "See you tomorrow."

She waved back while Eric pushed her out to the center of the ice. As he slowed to a stop and positioned the chair so it faced the frozen mountain, it began to snow — soft, giant flakes that drifted down from the midnight sky. Savannah looked up into the wintry darkness, tilting her head back to gaze at the beautiful white crystals drifting down to her. Lucy and Ellison slid closer and they all watched the snow in silence. Savvy caught a few icy flakes on her tongue and savored their watery coldness. There was no doubt about it — this was the best birthday ever.

CHECK OUT

The Sweetheart Deal

by Holly Kowitt

ANOTHER
CANDY APPLE BOOK . . .
JUST FOR YOU.

The teacher pointed to empty chairs. "Sit."

Madison cut him off. "Love to, can't. We're here to see if Fashion Club could use your room for —"

The words "Fashion Club" brought snickers.

"Oh." Brodkey's unibrow drooped. "Well, stick around for a minute. Meeting's almost over."

Oh, great. Now they were trapped!

Skyler and Madison exchanged horrified looks. Stick around for a . . . *Mathlete's meeting*? Skyler could see Madison deciding whether or not to blow it off. They both frowned. Neither wanted to let the other get points with Ashleigh.

"Big props to Madison!" Skyler imagined Ashleigh saying. "She got us Brodkey's room! GIVE HER SOME LOVE!" The club would roar with applause.

Skyler planted a studded hobo bag on a seat in the back row, and sat down. Her rivalry with Madison outweighed her horror of math geeks. Madison sighed and dumped her red patent leather purse on the chair next to her.

A glittery notebook fell out, and Madison grabbed it. Skyler recognized a slam book that had been going around school. People wrote in it anonymously, saying things that were too mean to say to someone's face. Madison opened the book and started writing furiously, flaunting her lack of interest in the scene around her. Well, if she wanted to be snarky, there was plenty of material here.

Turning her head, Skyler took in the view.

Whoa.

She saw white tube socks with clogs, cell phone holsters attached to belts, and a sea of unconditioned hair. The boy next to her wore a black calculator-watch the size of a baked potato.

"These people are freaks," Madison whispered, making a face.

"Shhhhhh," Skyler whispered back.

She had been only dimly aware of Mathletes, classifying such activities as Things of No Interest at Longbrook, along with the Recycling Club, science fair, and Salute to the Metric System assembly. Such events barely existed for her. Fashion Club, Pajama Day, the Valentine's Day Dance — these were the words splashed across Skyler's week planner in purple gel pen.

Skyler recognized a few people. Emily Berman, a spiky-haired, artsy-craftsy oddball who drew vegan-themed comics. Jasper Resnick, a mega-brain who always said, "Are you inputting that?" Adam Dowd, whose glasses were as thick as swimming goggles. A couple of others who belonged to the first-in-line-to-see-*The-Lord-of-the-Rings* crowd.

At the front of the room, a guy in a tuxedo T-shirt was talking. "Well, we stank at rational numbers," he said. "But in linear equations we're going to *kick butt.*"

"Sounds spazz-tastic," Madison whispered.

"I dunno." Skyler shrugged. "It's kinda cool they're so into it."

Actually, the scene was pretty interesting. *We go to the same school, but we inhabit a totally different universe,* thought Skyler. This world was right under her nose, but it had been invisible to her. Was her world as distant to them?

"Friday is our Pizza Pi party," said a girl in overalls and a tie-dyed thermal top. Skyler automatically gave her a mental makeover. A belted pink dress to make her waist look small, she thought. Over it, a classic black trench coat and matching cotton tights. Short-cropped high-heeled boots for height. Dangly silver earrings. A blunt bob haircut with straight bangs.

I'm good, thought Skyler. Inspired, she turned her attention to a guy wearing a *Battlestar Galactica* tee over long sleeves. She chose funky prep for him, a white button-down shirt over a rock band tee, and skater-boy long shorts. She trimmed his hair, rearranged his part, and put him in cool basketball shoes.

Not bad, thought Skyler.

She went around the room, assigning clothes to people. It was like playing with paper dolls. A mini-jumper to show off a petite frame. High-waisted pants to lengthen short legs. A green woven shirt to bring out gray eyes . . .

"That's it. Time for refreshments." Thermal Girl interrupted Skyler's thoughts. Finally! As the meeting broke up, she and Madison made a beeline for Mr. Brodkey. He was talking to a boy in a shirt that read I LIKE ANGLES — TO A DEGREE.

"Mr. Brodkey!" Skyler and Madison shouted in desperation.

"I'll catch up with you later, Taro." Brodkey turned to them. "How did you like Mathletes? Exciting stuff, huh?"

"Um —" Madison flashed a fake smile. "Totally. We were wondering if Fashion Club could use your room for a —"

"Too bad you missed the Mix 'N Math picnic," he continued.

"Bummer," said Skyler. "On February twenty-fifth, we —"

"I'll look at my calendar." He pointed to the snack table. "Graze."

Skyler and Madison checked out refreshments while they waited. "Even the snacks are nerdy," said Madison, plucking a Bugle chip from a plastic dish. She watched a guy walk by in a Death Star Tech Support T-shirt. "God. What. Losers."

Madison was really starting to bug her.

She and Skyler had a troubled history. At one time, they had been good friends, gossiping and raiding the mall together for free cheese samples. Madison was nicer then, showing her vulnerable side when her parents weren't getting along. It bugged Skyler that her friend turned against people so easily, but she chose to ignore it.

Then, at fifth grade summer camp, Madison

turned against Skyler. Everyone in the cabin ignored her — Madison's orders. Skyler was awkward then, tall for her age, and cursed with frizzy hair. Madison branded Skyler as uncool.

After a miserable summer, they finally made up — but never regained the same easy friendship. In the popular crowd, Skyler kept her distance from Madison. "Your frenemy," Julia called her. Madison was too powerful not to have as an ally, but she was too dangerous to be a real friend.

Meanwhile, Skyler grew into her height, straightened her hair, and discovered her inner fashionista. But her stint as a social outcast made her sensitive to people left out of the whirl.

"They're *not* losers." Skyler's voice rose. "They're just fashion-challenged."

"A dork's a dork." Madison spoke firmly. "You can't change that."

"Sure, you can." Now Skyler began to get angry. This was the kind of snobbish attitude that was ruining Fashion Club. "*Everyone* has potential, Madison."

"Yeah, right." Madison popped another Bugle.

"It's true!" Skyler waved a hand around the room. "Pick any guy here. I could make him so fierce, Ashleigh Carr would *beg* him for a Sweetheart Dance on Valentine's Day." The Sweetheart Dance was a turnabout moment at the school Valentine's Day Dance, when for one song, girls asked guys to dance.

Wow — did that really come out of her mouth?

"*Really?*" Madison raised an eyebrow. "The Valentine's Day Dance is in six weeks."

Skyler had been trying to make a point — not a serious offer. Was it really and truly *possible?* Skyler wasn't sure. If she really believed in the "power of fashion," this was her chance to back it up. She'd have to work fast. "I could do it," Skyler said, trying to muster confidence.

"Anyone?" Madison's eyes lit up.

"ANYONE." Skyler raised her chin.

Madison motioned for Skyler to turn around.

Behind her, a hooded figure in science safety goggles was talking loudly. Long hair peeked out from a purple plastic cape printed with WIZARDS & WARRIORS. A janitor's belt around his waist held a cell phone, PDA, pocketknife, and possibly, a wireless fax. To make matters worse, he was speaking in a fake robot voice.

He seemed to have missed several belt loops, so stonewashed jeans bunched up around his waist. The jeans also appeared to be hemmed. On his feet were white socks, stuffed into black leather Viking sandals.

Skyler stood watching, horrified but fascinated. The guy took nerdiness to a whole new level.

"The Green Goblin versus She-Hulk?" he was saying. "Not even CLOSE!"

Madison smiled sweetly.

"I pick *him*."

CANDY APPLE BOOKS

Drama Queen

I've Got a Secret

Confessions of a
Bitter Secret Santa

The Boy Next Door   The Sweetheart Deal

The Sister Switch

Snowfall Surprise

The Accidental
Cheerleader

The Babysitting Wars

Star-Crossed

read them all!

Accidentally
Fabulous

Accidentally
Famous

Accidentally
Fooled

Accidentally
Friends

How to Be a Girly Girl
in Just Ten Days

Miss Popularity

Miss Popularity
Goes Camping

Making Waves

Life, Starring Me!

Juicy Gossip

Callie for President

Totally Crushe-